A Highlander's Love

A Highlander's Love

By

Ronny Whitman

Love is two hearts connected as one, a soul-to-soul bond, gifted by God

Although this book mentions real people and places of history, this story is fully fiction, one of my own creation.

Prologue

Once they walked through the window of rebirth, Robert was born as Lord William Booth, the new Lord of Dunham Massey Castle, and Elizabeth was born ten years after Robert in the highlands of Inverness, as Lady Heather Campbell, far from England and the man she was bound to.

As Lord William and Lady Heather grew into young adults, both felt as if something was missing, a loss of some kind, but what it was, they didn't know. There were times when Lady Heather found herself looking south towards England, not realizing why, and Lord William, he too would find himself looking north towards Scotland, feeling there was something there he needed to find, what it was, neither of them knew.

With a great deal of land separating them, would Robert, as Lord William Booth, and Elizabeth, as Lady Heather Campbell, ever find each other again, or will the karma they created in their past life send them both on a different path? This would be tested when Lord William Booth received a message from his king ordering him to northern Scotland to speak to the highland lords to encourage them to sign his decree, giving up their lands to the English crown. In doing this, he hoped while he was in Scotland, he would discover what was calling to him.

Chapter 1

It was 1635 when Lord William Booth and his wife Lady Elizabeth Booth gave birth to their first-born child, a son, and the next Lord of Dunham Massey Castle. He was a strong and healthy boy with dark hair and brown eyes, and he was named William Booth the third.

As young Lord William grew to a young boy, he was adventurous and spent a great deal of time near the woods, but he was never allowed to venture any further beyond the forest tree line. Although he felt pulled to go further as if there was something he needed to see, unsure what it was, he was determined once he was a man, he would venture further into the woods hoping to discover what it was that was calling to him.

Once William was a young youth, he would go a short distance into the woods, but not as far as he wanted since his nursemaid was always near. He never understood why it was so important that he wasn't allowed to go further into the woods, not until much later when he learned of the story about young Elizabeth Massey and Robert Davenport, who once spent a great deal of time in those woods, and it was believed the woods were now haunted by their spirits, but young William never believed those stories to be true, yet he was never brave enough to find out. Unfortunately, it wouldn't be until much later after he was a man, having forgotten his need to venture into the woods since he was distracted by his duties to become the next Lord of Dunham Massey Castle.

Heather Campbell was born in the late 1600s, the daughter of Lord Campbell, and the first born, the eldest daughter of Clan Campbell. Her brother, who she cherished more than anything, was born ten years after her, which was also the day she lost her mother. From that day, Heather took on the role to help raise her brother, knowing it would be something her mother would have wanted her to do. Although she was from a high and noble family, it wasn't necessary to take on such a duty, but Heather could not leave her brother to be cared for by anyone other than herself. Her brother, who she named Sean, became everything to her. He was her heart, and the love she felt for her brother was more than a sister or a mother's love, but one of all, including friendship.

Many years when Sean was ten years old, he was out riding with his sister, racing across the meadow not far from the castle, when Sean's horse hoof hit a hole in the ground and tumbled over, throwing Sean through the air, and when he landed, his head hit a rock killing him instantly.

"Sean!" Heather called out as she jumped off her horse and ran to her brother. "Sean! Sean! Answer me!" When Heather reached her brother she grabbed him by his shoulders and tried to wake him, but he would not wake. She leaned down and listen to his chest, but she couldn't hear a heartbeat. "No, no, ye can no die. Ye can no leave me. Ye are all I have left of mother. Ye can no leave me too," she begged, but there was nothing she could do, Sean was gone.

Heather picked up her brother and laid him across his horse and once she was on her horse, she returned to the castle to tell her father that his only son was dead. "How do I tell da? Will he blame me for Sean's death?" shaking her head, "nae, father will no blame me. He will see it as the accident it was. He will grieve, but he will not blame me, no as I will blame myself." Heather turned to look at her brother with tears running down her face, "nae, tis my fault. I encouraged Sean to race me across the meadow, tis, I am to blame."

Heather rode back to the castle with sadness, as guilt was weighing down her heart, and when she returned to the castle, the guards saw Sean's body draped over the horse and they quickly rushed to help, believing he was only injured, but when they reached him, they saw he was dead. The captain looked at Heather for answers and she relayed what happened in the meadow.

"Quick, find the Laird!" called the captain of the guard. "Hurry men, help me carry him into the castle and up to his bedchambers."

The men with heavy hearts, did as their captain ordered and they slowly carried Sean into the castle and up to his bedchambers, where after a short time, Laird Campbell entered the room to find his son lying motionless on the bed.

"What happen to my son?" Laird Campbell asked.

"My Laird, there was an accident," he turned to look at Heather, and she was standing by the door with her head down and her hands crossed in front of her. "He was racing his horse in the meadow when the horse took a fall and was thrown from his horse, where he hit his head on a rock. My Laird, he is…no more."

Nae, no my son. My only son. How can ye take him from me now and so young? Nae, God, tell me tis no so? he thought, but he knew there was nothing God could do. Laird Campbell looked at his son with shock on his face, then at his daughter, and what he saw broke his heart even more. "Come child."

Heather slowly went to her father who embraced her in his arms and held her while she cried.

"My daughter, tis no yer fault. Tis an accident and nothing more."

Heather was shaking as she cried in her father's arms, then after a short time she heard, "Mary, come take Heather to her bedchamber and watch her carefully."

"Aye, My Laird, I shall stay with her." Mary took Heather from Laird Campbell's arms and helped her to her bedchamber.

Turning back to his son, "my son. How can I lose ye so soon? Ye was what was left of yer mother, but I know yer mother is with ye now. My love, my wife, take our son and care for him as ye would have done in life, ye can now do in death." Laird Campbell turned to the captain of the guard. "Call for the priest and prepare him…my son for burial," he said, then went and kneeled beside his son's bedside. "My son, ye will be remembered. Tis time ye go to be with yer mother. I love ye son.

I love ye, Sean." Laird Campbell lowered his head for a few moments, then kissed his son on the cheek, then stood and left the room.

Heather was lying on her bed crying uncontrollably with Mary sitting by her side, "hush child, tis alright. Tis no yer fault."

Aye, tis my fault! It tis my fault! Heather repeated in her mind over and over again.

Just then, her father walked in, "Mary, how is Heather."

"Oh, My Laird, she no do well. She has no stopped crying."

"Mary, give me a few moments alone with Heather. Go down and have cook fix her a plate of food and drink."

"Aye, My Laird." Mary curtsied, then left the bedchamber as she silently closed the door behind her.

Laird Campbell went and sat on the edge of Heather's bed. "Heather, my daughter, please no cry. Tis no yer fault. Tis was an accident and nothing more. Yer brother is now with yer mother."

Heather could not open her eyes, she couldn't bear to look at her father and see the shame in his eyes. She believed what he said, but she also knew his heart was breaking at the loss of his son and heir. Just then, Heather rose and embraced her father. "Oh da, tis my fault. I encouraged Sean to race me, if I no do this, he would no be dead. Aye, tis my fault," she said before she was overtaken by grief.

Laird Campbell knew it wasn't his daughter's fault, but right now there was nothing he could say that would change how she felt, so he did what he could, he held her in his arms until she cried herself to sleep.

Laird Campbell returned to his son's bedchamber, and when he did, he saw the priest standing over Sean's body giving him his last rights.

Once the priest was done, he turned to find Laird Campbell standing in the doorway. "My Laird, I am sorry about yer son. I have given him his last rights. When shall ye like to perform the wake?"

"On the fourth day. We shall have it in the great hall and bury him next to his mother in the family kirkyard."

"I shall make the arrangements. I will leave ye to mourn," the priest said and left the room.

After a few moments, Laird Campbell covered his son with his tartan, and after one more look, he too left the room.

On the day of Sean's wake, all of the clans, along with the people in Cawdor Village and the surrounding outskirt villages attended the laird's only son's wake. Those that could not fit in the great hall, stood outside waiting for Sean's body to be carried out and taken to the kirkyard to be buried. Laird Campbell was amazed by the number of people that came to pay their respects, and it pleased him to see how many of the people cared for and loved his son.

While Heather was getting ready for her brother's wake, her mind was running wild, *how can I do this? How can I see my brother lying dead? Tis my fault. Tis my fault. I no naught I can do this,* she thought, and the thoughts along with her grief were too much for her to bear, and she collapsed on the floor. "My Lady no. Lizzy, quick, go and bring the laird at once," hollard Mary.

Without waiting, Lizzy ran to find the laird.

"Ella, help me get Heather on her bed," said Mary.

Without another word, Ella and Mary carried Heather to her bed and just as they laid her down, Laird Campbell entered the room.

"What happened Mary!"

"Tis her grief My Laird. It was too much for her to bear."

"Let us leave her to rest, tis best she no attend her brother's wake and burial."

"Nae, My Laird. She will no forgive ye if ye let her miss her brother being put to rest. Give me time to revive her and I will bring her to ye."

Hesitant, Laird Campbell said, "very well Mary," then left the room.

After a few moments, Mary was able to revive Heather. "Oh, thank heavens. My Lady, do ye wish to go to the church?"

Groggy, Heather managed to say, "aye Mary, I do. I need to say goodbye to my brother. Will ye help me?" *Sean, I will no allow my grief to keep me from saying goodbye to ye.*

"Aye, My Lady, I will."

Mary helped Heather up and once she was steady, she helped her out of her bedchamber and down the stairs to the great hall. Once they entered, Heather's father was standing at her brother's coffin, and the sight of it caused her to swoon, but with Mary's help, Heather managed to make her way to her father's side.

When Laird Campbell saw his daughter come to be by his side, he smiled and put his arm around her. After the wake was over, the clan took Sean's coffin and carried it to the kirkyard where they laid his body to rest, and once the proceedings were over, Mary assisted Heather back to her bedchamber where she remained for five days. Although she will never forget her brother, it was time to live her life. Now that her father lost his son and heir, he would need her more than ever before, and she had to be strong for him.

Chapter 2

For the next twenty years, William grew to be a strong, dedicated, and caring man. Yes, he was the next Lord of Dunham Massey and was married to the great Lady Jane of Tatton Park, but even though his marriage was a happy union, for William, there was still something missing. What it was, he didn't know. Yes, he loved his wife and his home, but for some reason, it didn't feel right, as if something or someone was missing. His heart just wasn't in it. He wasn't connected to his wife as he should be, and he had this strange need to travel to Scotland, but that didn't make any sense, nor did he understand why.

When Lord Booth walked the grounds of Dunham Massey, there was something familiar about the place, even as a boy, he felt it, it felt – right. What it was he didn't know, not until the day he decided to walk further into the woods and came across a place, a lake he didn't know existed. Based on the look of it, it appeared he was the first to see this place in a long time, and as he walked towards the lake, his heart for the first time felt alive!

But why here and why now? he thought.

As he looked around there was something familiar and right about this place, *our sanctuary. Our safe haven.* "Why did I think that?" he whispered.

William felt confused and decided to sit on the old wooden bench that seemed to have been there for a very long time, and as he sat there, he staired out to the lake as he tried to understand why this place made his heart feel alive for the very first time in his life.

Jane would love this place, he thought, but then aloud, "NO!" he shouted.

William, without understanding why, the thought of Jane coming to this place felt wrong. So very wrong. *She does not belong here,* he thought.

"This place must be guarded and protected from others, even from my wife."

Shortly after, William stood and walked around the lake, coming almost to a full circle when he stopped at a spot near the lake that was a few feet from a tree, when something called to him, along with feeling a vibration directly under his boots, that seemed to pierce through the boots and was slowly making its way up his body, stopping in the center of his chest, directly over his heart.

William looked down as he tried to understand what was happening, and when he bent down to place his hand directly over the spot he was standing on – as soon as his hand touched the ground he was hit with an overwhelming amount of emotions and was shocked when he reached up to his face and found tears, which he quickly wiped away.

With curiosity, William pulled out his dagger and started digging at the spot when he heard footsteps. He quickly stood and turned to find a servant standing at the edge of the trees that surrounded the lake.

This place must be protected, he thought.

William became angry at the invasion of this place – his place. "Adam, what are you doing here!" he yelled.

Adam bowed and said, "forgive my intrusion, My Lord. Lady Booth sent me to find you."

Sighing, *of course, she did.* "No need Adam, I was about to return," William said, then turned and took another quick look back, and when he turned back to Adam, "tell no one of this place. Not even Lady Booth, do you understand?" he said, in a firm authoritative voice, one that was not to be questioned.

Adam bowed in understanding and said, "yes, of course, My Lord."

Together, William and Adam left the lake and returned to Dunham Massey Castle, but as if he couldn't help it, he looked back to the lake and the spot next to it, *I will return. I must,* he thought.

It's been two years since the death of her brother, and when the day came when Heather was called to her father's cabinet – she believed she knew what it was for, but she wasn't sure if she was ready, not so soon after losing her brother. Yes, it's been two years, but to her, if felt as if it happened yesterday. Was she ready to fulfill her father's wish? No, but she made a promise, and she must keep her promise no matter how she felt.

I must do this for da. Tis least I can do after causing the death of his only son and heir, she thought with a sigh.

The Campbells and the Keiths have been speaking for a long time regarding an agreement that will merge their clans through the marriage of Heather and Laird Keith's son William, after Heather's sixteenth birthday, until Heather managed to convince her father to wait until she was eighteen. Although he knew he shouldn't, Lord Campbell hesitantly agreed. He told himself he was doing this for his daughter, but deep down, he did it because he was not ready to let his daughter go. He loved his daughter more than life itself, and after he lost his son, his only heir, he found it too difficult to let her go. So, when Heather asked to postpone the wedding until she was eighteen, he happily agreed.

Now that she was eighteen and her father had requested to speak with her, she knew it was time to fulfill her promise to her father. As Heather approached her father's cabinet, she stopped just outside the door, needing a moment to gather herself for what she knew was to come. Heather took a deep breath and after she let it out, she walked into her father's cabinet.

"Da, ye wish to speak with me?"

Laird Campbell was sitting behind his desk with his head down working, but when he heard his daughter's voice, he quickly stopped and went to his daughter's side.

"Ah, Heather, aye, come," he said hugging his daughter. "Here, please sit," motioning to the chair next to him. "Heather, Laird Keith —"

Here we go, Heather thought, sighing.

"— is bringing his son to meet ye so we can formalize yer marriage contract, and once the contract is signed, we will announce to the clan of yer betrothal, then on the fourth night, we will travel to Dunnottar Castle in Stonehaven where ye will marry Lord William Keith."

Heather lets out a breath and said, "aye da, I will do as ye ask.

Laird Campbell knew this was not what his daughter wanted, but without an heir, they needed to build allies, and the Keith clan was a strong clan to have as an ally. Laird Campbell hugged his daughter, and after a few moments, she turned and left his cabinet and went to her favorite place in the woods, the one's that was located on the west side of Cawdor Castle.

Later that evening, Laird Campbell received a message from Laird Keith, informing him, although he could not go into detail, that something of great importance would prevent him from traveling to Cawdor Castle to finalize the marriage contract, and asked if Laird Campbell would be willing to travel to Dunnottar Castle a few days before the wedding was to take place, so they could finalize the marriage contract and shortly after, the wedding will take place.

Laird Keith, with understanding, immediately sent a response agreeing to Laird Keith's request.

When Connor was born, he was born as William Keith, but when he was just a small lad, he could con his nurse maids, kitchen hands, and at times, even the cook, to give him what he wanted. All he had to do was flash and flutter those puppy dog eyes of his, and they'd give him practically anything he asked for.

While he was in the kitchen waiting for his father, standing near the large center table that barely reached his head, forcing him to stand on his tip toes, he rested his chin on the edge of the table, and when the cook turned to look at him, he fluttered those puppy dog eyes of his.

When the cook Bertel saw William, at first, she was prepared to scull him and chase him out of her kitchen, but when she saw that little chin and his fluttering eyes, she couldn't help it, instead, she burst out laughing.

"Ye, young monster. Ye could get any lass with those eyes," she said.

Connor looked at Bertel and smiled, knowing he was going to get whatever he wanted.

"Ye, a little devil, ye are. At ye age, already a con-ner," she said, giving him what he wanted.

When William received the cookie he wanted, he smiled with satisfaction, and from that day fourth, he was called Connor by the servants, which caught on to the rest of the household and clan, and William was no longer called by his given name but became known as the little con-ner, that became his nickname Connor, to those closest to him, thus, William no longer existed, except for those who were stranger to them.

As Connor grew to be a man, he became a fierce and powerful warrior, one of the best swordsmen in his clan, and no one could beat him. A true highland warrior, one not to be reckoned with.

"Aye Connor, what are ye doing?" yelled Gordon.

"I am beating ye, tis what I am doing," Connor yelled over the clashing of swords.

"Aye, tis ye are, but we are only practicing. Ye are attacking as if we are in battle, and I am yer enemy."

"Aye, ye no want me to be easy on ye. I fight ye as if we are in battle, tis one day ye will be in battle and I need ye prepared for anything."

"Aye, tis so, but tis no today," Gordon said, then dropped to the ground and rolled under Connor, knocking his legs out from under him, causing Connor to stumble, but instead of falling as Gordon had hoped, Connor found his bearings and rightened himself.

"That is a wicked thing ye did Gordon."

Aye, but it worked, and I almost made ye fall on yer face. Tis would have been a great sight to be seen," Gordon said laughing.

Connor smiled, "aye, tis it would have been, but I am too good at what I do to be fooled by such a trick," Connor said with a smile.

"Aye, it seems ye are."

"Connor," yelled Laird Keith.

Connor turned when he heard his father, "aye da'."

"Come, we must speak."

"Aye. Gordon, continue practicing with the men while I speak to da'."

"Aye, as ye wish," Gordon said, then sprint off to the men still practicing a short distance from where they were.

"Come son, walk with me down to the shore," said Laird Keith.

Connor nodded and followed his father.

Once they were at the shoreline, "Connor, I have sent word to Laird Campbell, informing him we will not be able to travel to Cawdor Castle. I requested he come so we can formalize the marriage contract here before the wedding."

"Aye da', tis because of what ye heard about the English king sending a representative to force the lairds to give up their lands?"

"Aye son, tis is. I no want to leave Dunnottar if the information is true. Although the men are strong and can hold their own, tis best not to leave the castle without its laird."

"Aye da', I agree."

"Be ready son, for ye might find yer self in battle in the near future."

"Aye, I will be ready."

When Laird Campbell and Heather, along with the clan guards arrived at their first campsite after a long eight-hour ride, and while the men and servants were sitting up camp, Laird Campbell turned to his daughter, "Heather, how are ye child?"

Not looking at her father, but instead, she watched their tents being put up, "ah da, I am well, but ye know this is no easy for me."

"Aye, I do. We have no choice. We must continue to Dunnottar Castle to finalize the agreement between our two clans."

"Aye da, I am aware, but I am no happy about it. I will due my duty, as it is asked of me." *But tis the last thing I wish to do, is to marry a man I no love,* she thought with a long sigh.

Laird Campbell went to his daughter and put his arms around her, "daughter, ye will do yer clan and me a great honor by doing yer duty to yer clan."

"Aye, da. Aye."

Once the tents were ready, Laird Keith went to his and Heather went to hers, where they cleaned and dressed for the evening meal before retiring for the night.

The following morning at sunrise, they began their journey again, a journey that would take them four days before reaching the outskirts of Dunnottar Castle landing them in Stonehaven.

When Laird Campbell and Heather arrived at Stonehaven, Heather had her first glimpse of Dunnottar Castle as it sat on the edge of a cliff overlooking the sea – it was breathtaking.

Tis is my new home? Aye, tis is beautiful. "Da, tis beautiful," Heather said with awe.

"Aye, tis is. I think ye will be very happy here," he said with a smirk.

As Laird Campbell and Heather traveled through the thick forest to Dunnottar Castle, and once they reached the outskirts of the castle, it gave them their first glimpse of the massive castle rising before them like a unpintratral fortress rising from the ashes of hell. At first, it frightened Heather, as it didn't appear to be the castle she saw from Stonehaven.

As they continued to get closer, she saw there was a large wall that surrounded the castle, protecting it from unwanted visitors. Once the guard waved them pass, Heather was amazed by the beauty of the place, and she immediately fell in love with it. *This is going to be my home,* she thought. She always believed her home at Cawdor Castle was beautiful, but this, this castle, and its surroundings were breathtaking.

Laird Campbell was watching his daughter's reaction very carefully when she saw Dunnottar Castle, and after a short time he said, "this will no be a bad union, aye?"

Heather looked at her father and smiled, "aye, no bad. If I no love the son, I can love his land," she said with a laugh, "tis breathtaking."

"Aye, tis is. I think ye shall love living at Dunnottar Castle," he said smiling.

Once they were beyond the great gates of Dunnottar Castle, and arrived at the stables, as they were dismounting, they were immediately greeted by Laird Keith and his son William.

Laird Keith bowed as he said, "ye are very welcome, Laird Campbell and Lady Heather. My Lady, may I introduce ye to my son and yer betrothal, Lord William Keith, but we, the clan, call him Connor," he said with a wicked smile, "a story I am sure ye will find quite amusing and something I am sure Connor will be happy to tell ye," turning to his son as he gave him a wicked smile.

Connor looked at his father and sighed, "aye da', I am sure Lady Heather will find it very amusing," he said with mockery.

Laird Keith just smiled at his son.

Heather, not understanding what was happening between Laird Keith and his son, curtsied, and said, "I am pleased to meet ye," smiling at Larid Keith, then she looked at Connor, *tis, he is a handsome man, but does he have a good heart?* "I look forward to hearing the story of how ye came to be called Connor?" she said with a smile.

When Connor first saw Heather, he couldn't believe his good fortune, she was beautiful. She had long beautiful curly orange-red hair with the brightest of green eyes, as bright as an emerald. Connor looked at his father, then back at Heather, "My Lady," he said bowing, "I shall be more than happy to tell ye the tale of how my name came to be."

As Heather watched the interaction between Connor and his father, she couldn't help but notice how handsome he was. He had long dark wavy hair and chocolate brown eyes, and she couldn't help but notice his broad shoulders and his chest was strong and firm. A warrior's body. Her body warmed at the sight of him.

Turning her attention back to the conversation, "then I shall look forward to hearing it," she said with a smile, and then was surprised at the flutters she felt in her stomach. It surprised her to find that she liked him, something she did not expect. *Aye, tis good,* she thought.

Laird Keith and Connor led the way to the great hall where they sat to go over the marriage contract, at the same time, to allow Connor and Heather the time to get to know each other.

With the contract signed, Laird Keith and Laird Campbell turned to Connor and Heather and were pleased to see the conversation between them was going well.

"Tis a funny story of how ye came to yer name," Heather said with laughter.

"Aye tis is," he said, then to change the subject, "aye, the ride to Dunnottar is no an easy one. I am glad ye made it safe," Connor said.

"Aye, I will no want to do it again for a long time If I could manage it," Heather said with a slight smile.

Connor laughed, "aye, I can understand what ye mean."

For Heather, she was surprised at how easy it was to talk to Connor – as if she was talking to someone she's known all her life. It felt comfortable and it felt right. As Heather watched Connor, she thought, *yes, I can. I can love him.* This, she had no doubt.

When Connor first saw Heather there was an immediate connection, but as he talked to her, it was as if his heart started beating for the first time in his life, and he knew just then he could easily love her – he did love her, but how could that be, when they were just getting to know one another. As he was looking at this beautiful woman he wondered, *could she love me as well?*

As Heather and Connor were looking at each other from across the table with their Da's on each side of them, Heather smiled at Connor, and he at her – there was no doubt they could love each other, and their hearts sang at the wonderful future that beheld them.

Since Heather was born into highland nobility, she had a responsibility, one she had no control over, but when she saw Connor, she knew she was destined to be bound to this man she never met until now. Before she met Connor, she wasn't sure she could ever give him her heart, or any man, but to her surprise, for the first time upon seeing him, her heart sang with pleasure, telling her he was the one. The one she was meant to be with – to love. Was it possible she can truly love this man, a stranger she had only recently met, the man who will soon be her husband? This, she could not know or understand.

As Laird Keith and his son were sitting at the long table in the great hall across from Laird Campbell and his daughter, he didn't miss the look between his son and Heather, and thought, *tis will be a great union,* then gave a small smirk.

Chapter 3

Heather was in her borrowed bedchamber that was given to her by Laird Keith, lying on her bed as she thought, *never could I have believed that this arranged marriage could end up with me loving the man…my betrothal, and after a short time from our meeting, in seeing him and his handsome face.* She gave a slight smile. *God help me, I do, I love Connor Keith. Just the thought of it makes my heart swell, and to think, I did no want this. Now, after being in his company and seeing him for the first time, I do, I want it so terribly.*

The thought of marrying Connor Keith was more than she ever dreamed of. Heather knew she'd marry, but never did she believe it would be for love, but instead for honor and duty to her family and clan. To feel love for Connor, was more than she ever hoped for.

In the middle of Heather's thoughts, she heard a knock on her door, "Come," she said.

When the door opened, a servant girl walked in, and once the door was closed, she curtsied and said, "My Lady, yer father requests ye to come to his bedchamber. He wishes to speak with ye."

Heather smiled; she knew what her father wanted to speak to her about. He wanted to know what she thought of Connor. "Oh, very well. Thank ye."

The girl curtsied and quickly left Heather's bedchamber. Heather stood from the bed and gave herself a quick look in the mirror, and after she straightened her gown and righted her hair, she left her bedchamber and headed to see her father.

Once Heather arrived at her father's bedchamber door, she knocked.

"Enter," Laird Campbell said.

When Heather heard her father, she opened the door and went in. "Da, ye wish to speak with me?"

Laird Campbell turned when he heard his daughter, "aye, Heather," he said reaching out his hand, "come to me."

Without hesitation, Heather quickly went to her father and placed her hand in his, and when she did, her father pulled her into his arms. "My daughter, what did ye think of Connor? Can ye marry him? Maybe, even love him?" he asked with hope in his heart.

Heather smiled, "aye da…I think," lowering her eyes, "I already love him," then she looked at her father and smiled with a sparkle in her eyes, "there is something about him tis make my heart jump at the sight of him."

For Laird Campbell to hear this, gave him great joy with a feeling of relief, "ah, Heather, tis makes me happy, and tis will be easier to let ye go. To know ye will love Connor, as I can clearly see he admires, and possibly loves ye as well, will ease my heart to know I will be leaving ye in good hands."

Heather hugged her father and said, "aye da and thank ye."

Once Laird Campbell and his daughter left the great hall to their bedchambers, Laird Keith turned to his son and asked, "well son, what do ye think of the lass?"

Connor reluctantly and slowly turned away from staring at the door Heather disappeared through, to look at his father and with a smile, "I already love the lass da. There is something about her that sent my heart soaring. Thank ye da, for my betrothal. She is a find beauty, and I can honestly say I have already given her my heart."

Laird Keith smiled at his son and said, "well son, looks like we made a good alliance, aye."

Connor only smiled at his father. A wide smile that filled his face, and for Laird Keith to see this, he slapped Connor on the back, then ordered a servant to bring them ale so they could celebrate his son's upcoming wedding.

Later that evening, while Connor was in his bedchamber sitting on his chair that was situated near the window, his thoughts were consumed by the lass – his lass, who was to be his bride – his wife.

I love her already. How is this possible? Just thinking of her makes my heart swell. I had a duty to my clan, and I was prepared to marry the lass out of honor and duty, but never did I believe I would be marrying for love. I do, I love the lass…Heather. My Heather.

These thoughts brought a smile to Connor's face, with a feeling of great joy and pride at his luck in finding love with an arranged marriage, a rare one at that, to be one of the few lucky ones, as his father was, to find love made his heart swell even further with pride.

The following morning as anxious as he was, Connor stood at the bottom of the stairs waiting to greet Heather when she came down for morning meal, and when he first laid eyes on her as she started down the stairs, she was even more beautiful than he recalled from the night before.

"Good morrow Heather," he said with a bow, then put his hand out to her, "did ye sleep well?" As Heather took his offered hand, Connor leaned in and kissed her on the cheek. "May I escort ye to morning meal?"

When Heather reached the first landing of the stairs, she was surprised to see Connor waiting for her at the foot, and at the same time, it pleased her, as it brought her great joy at seeing him waiting for her. When she woke that morning, she couldn't wait to dress and make her way down to morning meal so she could see him. Now, to see Connor waiting for her at the foot of the stairs, caused her heart to jump at the sight of him.

"Aye," she said as she curtsied. "I slept well, and ye?"

"Aye, well indeed. After morning meal, I would like to show ye around Dunnottar Castle and our wonderful village of Stonehaven. Will ye accompany me lass?" he said with sincerity and hope in his voice.

With a broad smile, Heather looked up at Connor, "aye, Connor, tis would please me very much. I thank ye."

"Come, let us go to morning meal."

Heather and Connor together went to have morning meal, and when they arrived in the great hall, her father and Laird Keith were already at the table along with many of the Keith and Campbell clan having their morning meal, which consisted of hot porridge and oak bread.

"Good morrow daughter, Connor," Laird Campbell said.

"Good morrow Connor and Heather," Laird Keith said.

Connor and Heather took a seat at the table directly in front of their fathers, and once they were seated, they were immediately given hot porridge and bread along with hot ale.

"Did ye sleep well," asked Laird Keith.

"Aye, very well," Connor and Heather said at the same time, then burst out laughing.

"Aye, we did da," said Connor.

"Aye da," said Heather.

Connor and Heather looked at each other and smiled, and when Laird Campbell and Laird Keith saw this, they looked at each other and smiled. This arrangement was going to be one of love, not honor and duty to their clans, and this pleased them both.

Once morning meal was over, Connor took Heather's arm and placed it in the crook of his, and together they left the great hall and Connor began her tour in the courtyard. As they stood at the cistern, Connor, with his arm pointed at the cistern, "this is where we receive most of our water for all our needs. We have another place further down, but if we were ever under siege, it would be very difficult to reach. As ye saw when ye arrived, we are situated well, protected by the cliffs, mountains, and the sea."

Heather looked at the cistern for a moment, then looked around at where they were, it was a remarkable place, situated high on the cliff, overlooking the magnificent sea that stretched beyond what the eye could see. Although she couldn't see the sea from where they were standing, she could hear the power of the waves crashing against rocks and land below. And above their heads, towards the cliffs nearby were a massive number of birds.

"Connor," Heather said, pointing at the birds off in the distance that were flying around, "what are those birds?"

Connor looked in the direction Heather was looking, "ah, those are puffins. They are excellent fishermen, as they can grab several fish in their bills. Tis fascinating to watch." Turning to Heather, "would ye like to go and watch? There is a place," pointing his figure at a cliff on the north side of the castle, "and watch them?" he asked.

Heather turned to look at Connor, "nae, no this time. Please continue showing me Dunnottar Castle," she said with a sly smile.

"Aye, we have plenty of time.

Looking around, seeing how well-fortified the castle was, Heather had no doubt she would be well-protected here. Turning back to the cistern, "tis beautiful, but will no the water run out?" she said with awe.

"No, it will never run dry. No with all the rain we receive. If it were to run dry, we can obtain water, although it would be with great difficulty, it can be done. In all my yer's, this cistern has never gone dry," he said, looking down at Heather with a smile. "Shall we continue," he asked gesturing with his arm to the south side. Heather nodded, and they headed to that side of the castle wall. "Here is where some of the servants reside, along with our officers," he said, then turned towards the sea on the east side of the wall, "as ye see," directing his arm toward the church, "tis is the church we will be married in," he said, smiling with anticipation.

"Tis beautiful Connor. Dunnottar Castle is one of the most beautiful castles I have ever seen, except for Cawdor Castle," she said with a slight smile.

"Aye, I am sure it is. I am sure I will see it one day."

Heather turned to look at Connor, and with a smile, "aye, ye will."

"Come," Connor said taking Heather's elbow as he guided her towards the servant's quarters. Waving at the west side of the castle, "tis the servant quarters. Come, I will show ye the family kirkyard, which was a large courtyard with a wonderful view of the sea.

When Heather saw the sea, it took her breath away, "Connor, tis beautiful, to see far out to the sea," she said, turning in a complete circle, wanting to take it all in, as she listened to the sea crashing against the rocks below. Then, something caught her eye, it was a cliff on the south side of the castle near the forest tree line, and for some reason, one she didn't understand, the place captivated her.

"Connor, can we go there," she asked pointing at the cliff.

Connor smiled when he saw what she was pointing at. *Ah, she spotted my favorite place,* he thought.

"My Lady, but of course, tis my favorite place to go when I wish to be alone. We shall go there once we finish our tour of the castle."

"Nae Connor, the castle is beautiful, but I wish to go there now," she asked, turning to look directly into his eyes, which took his breath away. "If ye no mind," she asked demurely.

Unable to resist her, Connor put out the crook of his arm, and once she put her arm in his, he guided her to a back entrance that took them down a few steps, then up a steep hill until they reached the path that led to the cliff on the other side of the castle.

Once they reached the cliff, Heather slipped her arm from Connor's and went to stand at the edge of the cliff and looked down to the water and rocks below, then to the sea beyond, where again it took her breath away. She placed her hand over her heart, "Connor, tis beautiful. I can see why ye love this place. If ye no mind, I wish this place to be my favorite place as well," she said, then turned to look at Connor.

The look Heather gave him, was like a punch to his chest, stealing the breath from him. Connor couldn't help it, he had to – he slid his hand down the side of her face in a soft caress. "Love, this brings me great joy to share my favorite place with ye, ye who will be my wife."

Heather shivered at Connor's touch, causing her heart to race, and when she looked up at him, and her eyes met his, she saw something she didn't believe possible – *tis true, tis love I see in his eyes.* Heather smiled at Connor, to see his love for her in his eyes filled her with joy and anticipation – will he kiss her?

Just then, as if Connor read her mind, he slowly lowered his head, giving Heather a chance to pull away, and when she didn't, he lightly touched his lips to hers, and when she still didn't pull away, he kissed her.

Heather could not believe he was going to kiss her, causing her heart to race. She felt nervous, and scared, yet excited at the same time. He gave her a chance to pull away, but she didn't want to, she wanted him to kiss her, and when his lips touched hers, it took her breath away, and she allowed herself to fall into his kiss as his arms tighten around her.

Sensing her acceptance, Connor turned his soft and gentle kiss, into a more aggressive and deeper one, as he pulled her into his arms, feeling the softness of her body tight against his.

When Connor broke the kiss, they were breathing heavily, loss of all breath. "Heather, will it scare ye if I told ye I love ye? I know we only met but a day ago, but my heart recognizes ye as belonging to me. Ye are my love."

Heather smiled with joy at Connor's declaration. "Nae, Connor, my heart also recognizes ye, I too…love ye. Tis too soon, I know, but ye are already in my heart. How is this possible, I no understand?"

Filled with great joy, Connor pulled Heather tighter into his arms, wanting to enjoy the feel of her body against his, as she wanted the feel of his strong hard body against hers, and together they stood there for a long while before Connor gestured to return to the castle where they obtained two horses and continued to the village of Stonehaven.

Chapter 4

It was a week before Connor and Heather's wedding when Laird Keith received a visit from an English lord on behalf of the English King.

When William reached Stonehaven and saw Dunnottar Castle sitting high and on the edge of the sea, he saw a formidable castle. The closer he approached the outer walls of Dunnottar Castle, he was surprised to see what looks to be an impenetrable fortress. *Ah, I can see why the king would desire such a place,* William thought. Once William reached the gates of Dunnottar Castle, he informed the guard who he was, and once he was granted permission to enter, he was greeted by Laird Keith when he reached the stables.

"Ye are very welcome, Lord Booth."

"Good day, Laird Keith. Thank you. I have come on behalf of the English king to discuss your lands."

The rumors are true then, Laird Keith thought. "Lord Booth, I do no understand yer purpose or what the English have to do with my land, but as a noble Lord, I invite ye into my home and will hear what ye have to say."

Lord Booth bowed to Laird Keith, "Thank you, My Lord."

Laird Keith guided Lord Booth to the great hall where his son and his soon-to-be daughter-in-law, along with Laird Campbell were waiting.

Upon Lord Booth entering the great room, Heather was startled by the sight of the man, causing her heart to race, beating with such vigor, as if it came alive for the first time, which shocked her. She believed when she first saw Connor, was the first time her heart came alive. So, what did this mean? Why was she having such feelings for this stranger – this English lord, but not in the same way as it did with Connor, it was stronger – deeper. What was she to do, and how was she to act to such feelings?

"Lord Booth, allow me to introduce ye to my son William Keith, Laird Campbell from Cawdor Castle, and his daughter, who is my son's betrothed, Lady Heather Campbell. They are due to be married in five days hence.

"Good evening," Lord Booth said as he bowed. When he saw Heather, he heard the word *home* echo in his mind. And when their eyes met, there was a recognition between them both, and it was clear, she felt what he was feeling. What was to be done, he was a married man, and she was soon to be married to Laird Keith's son and heir.

Heather just met Connor, and she already felt – she believed she loved him, but after seeing Lord Booth and the way he made her feel, she wasn't sure if she could ever fully give Connor her heart. It shamed her since she didn't understand why she felt this way or why she believed this man, this stranger, this Lord Booth, already owned her heart. She needed time to think, time to understand what she was feeling.

Heather quickly stood, "excuse me, but I shall leave ye men to yer business," she said, then turned to Connor, "love, I shall go for a walk. I will see ye before I retire for the evening." With reluctance, she turned to Lord Booth, "tis a pleasure to meet ye Lord Booth. Good evening," she said as she curtsied, then turned and quickly started to leave the room.

Laird Campbell called to his daughter, "aye, a moment Heather," he said, as he stood and went to speak to his daughter, "Heather, are ye well?" he asked.

"Aye, da, I am well. I feel that this is man's business and there is no need for me to remain here, and I feel the need for the night's fresh air."

"Aye, very well. Make sure ye stay in sight of the guards."

"Aye da, I shall," she said, then kissed her father on the cheek and turned and left.

As Lord Booth watched the interaction between Laird Campbell and his daughter, his heart was racing, and his foot started to move forward, with the need to chase after her, but he quickly stopped before he made a fool of himself. Whatever he was feeling, he had to remember she was to be married and he too was a married man, but then he thought, *it should be me,* with a feeling of jealousy.

Before Heather was out of the room, Lord Booth said, "My Lady, it is an honor to meet you. I wish you many years return on your upcoming marriage."

Heather stopped, remembering her manners, as her heart was racing, with the need to turn and run, instead, she said, "tis a pleasure to meet ye Lord Booth, and thank ye on yer well wishes." Heather curtsied, then quickly left the room.

Laird Campbell turned back, and with Lord Booth, together they returned to the table, while Heather quickly made her way out of the castle, with her need to clear Lord Booth from her mind and to understand what she was feeling. Heather didn't go to her and Connor's favorite place, but instead, she went in the opposite direction and found herself on the cliff on the north side of the castle, opposite from her and Connor's favorite place.

"Lord Booth, tell us what brings ye to my land?" Laird Keith asked.

"I received a letter from the king of England, requesting that I come to Scotland, to visit all the highland lairds, and request they relinquish their lands to your king."

My king, I think no, Laird Keith thought, looking at Laird Campbell, it was clear, he was thinking the same as he was.

The highlanders and some of the lowlanders never accepted the new English king as their king, but instead, they were determined to remove this king from power.

"Why would we," Laird Keith said, turning his attention back to Lord Booth, "give up our land to 'yer' king?"

Lord Booth did not miss the emphasis of 'yer' and continued to explain, "King Charles needs your land, especially this land and castle as it is well fortified against the sea, which will help against the French."

"Aye, tis true, but why would I give King Charles my land and castle? I and my men can easily defend this place. We no need the English," Laird Keith asked.

"I understand what you are saying, but my request is only a courtesy. If you were to refuse to relinquish your land and castle, then the king will send in his soldiers and take them from you. I do not wish to see that happen."

At what Lord Booth said, Laird Keith, became outraged, "ye think yer soldiers are powerful enough to remove me and my clan from my land!" he roared as he stood, along with Laird Campbell.

"Forgive me, I do not wish to upset you, I am only here to relay the message from our king to you and the other Lairds of the highlands. Before you rush to your decision, take time to think about what it would mean to your people…clan if you were to refuse."

Laird Campbell put his hand on Laird Keith's arm, an indication for them to discuss this without the English lord. "Very well, I will sleep on it and let ye know on the morrow," Laird Keith said, then singled for one of his men to escort Lord Booth to a bedchamber. "Take Lord Booth to a bedchamber for the evening," he said, then turned to Lord Booth, "I bid ye good evening," then turned his back on him.

Lord Booth took the hint and stood from the table, he bowed to both lairds, then turned and followed the man to a bedchamber at the top of the stairs. However, once he was in his room and saw his belongings sitting on the bed, he felt too restless to go to bed, so Lord Booth turned to the man that escorted him to his chambers and asked, "I would like to take a walk before I retire for the night."

"Very well. Follow me."

Lord Booth followed the man until they were outdoors, where the man pointed in the direction north of the castle, "ye may walk in that direction, but do no go any further. There are guards all around watching ye."

Lord Booth looked around and saw men stationed all around the castle and on the walls that surrounded the castle. "Thank you. I will keep to the path," he said, bowing to the man, then turned and headed down the path.

As he walked with no particular direction in mind, he found himself walking in the direction of the cliff that was on the north side of the castle, with his mind racing with what happened with Laird Keith and Laird Campbell, but most of all, with Lady Heather. He respected the two lairds, and it bothered him on what he was there to do. Although it didn't go as well as he expected, nor was he surprised by their reaction, he had a job to do for king and country.

He felt restless, being unable to get Heather out of his mind, and the only way he knew to clear his mind, was to take a long walk to deal with these strange feelings he was having for this woman he didn't know. She was a beautiful woman who stirred things in him he didn't know existed. As he walked, he shook his head, unable to rid his mind of this woman, and when he reached the place that took him to the cliff, he was surprised to find Lady Heather standing at the edge of the cliff with her hair blowing in the wind, and the sight of her caused his heart to jump and he nearly tripped over his own two feet.

William was a man, a warrior, who didn't take things lightly. Assessing his surroundings as a warrior should. This night – this night, he was not the warrior, but a man who didn't know who or what he was. How this woman, for some reason, one he didn't understand, owned his heart and soul. But why? And why now? Why did he feel this way? He was married to a wonderful woman who he loved very much, so, why now and with this Scottish woman who was to be married? Although he loved his wife, he had always felt something was missing, was this the reason – this Scottish woman? Shaking his head, *I am losing my mind.*

He was an English lord, sent to negotiate with Laird Keith to hand his lands to the crown, and when he laid his eyes on Lady

Campbell, a highlander lady, who was about to wed a highlander lord, who will one day be Laird of Dunnottar Castle, a man she believed she loved with all her heart, but he believed it was he, that she should love with all his heart and no other.

As he watched the woman standing before him who had been occupying his mind, he knew the right thing to do was to turn away and leave, but his feet would not move, instead, they began moving toward her.

Heather didn't know how long she was standing on the edge of the cliff when she heard a noise, and when she turned around, she expected to see Connor but was surprised to see Lord Booth instead, the man who'd been occupying her mind.

"Tis ye," she said with shock. Then, there were flashes of a young English woman with a young English man holding each other at a lake in a forest. With sudden recognition, and without delay, she rushed towards Lord Booth.

At the same time, Lord Booth also had memories of a man and a woman from a time past, in the place he recently discovered, and with this sudden recognition, he rushed towards Heather, and once they were only a few feet away, he said, "it is you. I cannot believe it is you." The shock at seeing this woman, the woman he once loved, was overwhelming. Without waiting any further, William took Heather in his arms and held her in a tight embrace. Before he came to Scotland, he felt lost, but with Heather in his arms, all felt right – they were together once again. "Come away with me," William said.

Heather could not believe what she was doing – feeling. He was the one who held her heart and soul. The one she believed she'd been waiting for all her life. When Lord Booth asked her to go away with him, she wanted to say yes but knew she could not. How was she to say the words she knew would destroy them both?

Lord Booth didn't miss Heather's hesitation, and he needed to find a way to change her mind. "You must. We are meant to be together," he said, as all rational thought left him, forgetting he was already a married man, and she was about to be married. How could they possibly be together? At that moment, none of that mattered. The only thing that mattered was being with this woman – Heather.

"Yes, yes, forever more," she cried, also, forgetting all rational thought, thinking nothing of Connor, and with that, Lord Booth kissed her with such passion, a passion he's never felt when he was with his wife, a feeling he seemed to have recognized. A feeling he believed was lost to him forever.

With a sudden realization of where and who she was, Heather stopped and pushed Lord Booth away from her. "What am I doing? No I can no do this. I love Connor. We are to be married. I can no go with ye. No I can no!" she yelled, as panic set in, and without waiting for Lord Booth to respond, she pulled away and ran from him, leaving him feeling bereft.

Connor? Who is this Connor, William thought. Then, realization dawned on him, *it must be a nickname.*

When Heather pulled away and fled from him, William felt as if his heart was being ripped out of his chest as if there was one side of a string tied to his heart and the other to hers, and when she fled, she ripped out a piece of his heart, leaving behind a hole that will never be filled. He knew what he did was wrong, after all, she was to be married, and he was a married man. He knew he should not have done what he did – William, turned to look out at the sea, *I must leave this place at once. After what just happened, I cannot force these people to give up their land. It is wrong. I must find a way to help these people…save them from Cromwell,* he thought, feeling such shame, as it washed over him like an ocean wave. *Jane, I am so sorry I have betrayed my vows to you. I promise you…I will make right the weakness I felt this night.* William turned away from the cliff and quickly made his way back to the castle, once he was sure Heather was long gone. *I will leave before dawn. Before she is awake. I cannot bear to see her again. I do not know what I would do if I did.*

Once Lord Booth returned to the castle, he went directly to his bedchamber and order his servants to have everything ready for them to leave before dawn in the morning, as he thought about Heather's last words to him, *I know who ye are, but I can no hurt Connor…William, nor can I betray my father and clan.* When she returned just as he was about to leave the cliff. He hated leaving her alone on the cliff, but he promised to leave as soon as he could.

Chapter 5

When Connor woke the following morning, he decided to search for Heather. The night before, when he learned Heather retired to her bedchamber without seeing or saying good night to him disturbed him.

He started with her bedchambers, and when he didn't receive an answer to his knock, he slowly opened the door, and when he looked inside she was nowhere to be found, so he looked for her in the great hall, and when she wasn't there, he became concerned, and decided to search the entire castle, until he finally found her in the kitchen sitting on the cellar floor with her chin resting on her knees.

"Heather lass, what are ye doing in this wee cellar sitting on the floor?" he asked.

Heather raised her head to look at Connor, and she shook her head, "please Connor, leave me to my thoughts. I am so confused and do no what to do." *Or do I,* she thought. As she looked at Connor, *I love him so. How could I…*she stopped, unable to continue with that thought.

When Heather raised her head, Connor saw the pain and anguish in her eyes. She was suffering, but he didn't know why. He entered the cellar – it was a small and narrow room, and once he was standing in front of her, he knelt on the floor so he could be at her level.

"Heather, love, what has caused ye so much pain that ye come here to hide, even from me, yer man?"

Heather shook her head, as she placed her face between her knees to hide her face. "No, Connor, I can no speak of it, especially no to ye. Please, Connor, leave me," she said looking up at him with pleading in her eyes.

"Heather love, ye know I will no leave ye when ye are suffering so. Tell me, lass, tell me what is ailing ye? Ye know there is nothing ye can tell me that will cause me to think ill of ye," he said, as he carefully and gently placed his hands over hers.

In a muffled voice, Heather said, "no Connor, no this. This, I can no tell ye."

"Heather love, ye know there is nothing ye can no tell me, yer man, yer soon to be husband. Please love, tell me what has caused ye so much pain?"

Connor wanted nothing more than to pull Heather into his arms, but from what he saw, he knew it was the wrong thing to do. He needed to be patient and allow Heather time to confide in him on her own.

It was killing Heather having Connor be so gentle to her, but if he knew the reason for her pain, how would he react then? Would he hate her? Refuse to marry her? Or worse, would he go after Lord Booth and demand a duel to protect her honor? Although she did nothing that would require him to protect her honor, she still feared it.

"Connor," she said in a muffled voice, "ye no naught what ye ask of me."

"Love, if we are to marry, there nae…no be secrets between us. Love, please, tell me? Ye are worrying me, love."

At this, there was a noise in the kitchen, from the cook and kitchen help arriving to prepare the morning meal. Connor reached for Heather's hand again, "love, no here. Come, let us go to a place that will give us privacy."

Heather looked up at Connor with tears in her eyes, and for Connor to see this, it broke his heart. It only made him more determined to get to the bottom of what was happening. "Come, love, ye know ye can no stay here."

Heather firmly gripped Connor's hand and nodded, allowing him to help her up. As she rose, she asked, "where are we to go? No to our place. I could no bear to tell ye this there."

To hear this, caused Connor's heart to race, and tighten, as fear engulfed him. *What could she say that she could no say at our place? The place she…we love.*

Connor, with care, slowly asked, "where do ye wish to go, lass?"

Heather was watching Connor carefully, looking for a sign of what he was thinking, and when she saw him stiffen, she placed her hand on his arm and said, "let us go. I feel trapped. Let us go outdoors."

Connor placed Heather's hand in the crook of his arm and guided her out of the cellar. "Shall we go to the edge of the castle walls then?" he asked, looking down at her. With a nod of her head, they left the cellar, ignoring the looks they knew they were receiving from the kitchen staff, but the staff knew their place, and dare not say a word.

Once Connor and Heather were at the west side of the castle wall, with the sea just on the other side, he took her in his arms with the need to hold and comfort her.

For Heather to be in Connor's arms, felt so good and right, and then shame washed over her, causing her to quickly pull away from him, and when he wouldn't budge, she placed her hands on his chest and pushed him away from her. "No, Connor. Please, I do no deserve yer comfort." When Connor was about to speak, she placed her hand up, stopping him from doing so. "Nae. Ye must allow me to speak. To tell ye, without ye speaking, no until I have finished," she said.

Connor only stared at Heather, looking into her eyes searching for some telling sign that would tell him what she was going to say, but saw nothing, and without words, he nodded in agreement.

Heather took a deep breath, and for a moment, she had to turn away from him, and when she let it out, she squared her shoulders and braced herself for Connor's response, which she was sure to receive when he hears her confession.

When Heather turned back to face Connor, she looked directly into his eyes and said, "Connor, I am no the woman ye believe me to be. I have shamed ye," she said, then stopped to take another deep breath, and after releasing it, she looked at

Connor and noticed him stiffen, and how uneasy he was, even more so not knowing what she was about to tell him.

Seeing the guilt on Heather's face, Connor's fear grew, and he wondered, *what could she have done, for her to feel fear and shame.* Although Connor wanted to speak, he honored his agreement and remained silent, allowing Heather to say what she needed to say.

"Connor, first allow me to tell ye, I love ye with all my heart and soul. No matter what I say, tis important ye know this. I want nothing more than to become yer wife." At this declaration, Heather could see Connor relax a little, but now – now was the time for the truth. "Connor, the English, Lord William Booth, well…" she started to speak the truth but stopped. She had to close her eyes, to brace herself for Connor's reaction to what she was about to tell him.

What could this Lord…what could she say? he thought as he stiffened again, knowing this time he didn't hide his reaction from Heather.

Heather saw Connor stiffen again, but it didn't deter her. What she had to say, needed to be said. "During my and yer da's meeting with the English Lord, I went for a walk as I always do, and after much time had passed, I was standing on the cliff just over there," she pointed to the place that was north of where they were standing. "I believed I was alone when I heard a noise, and when I turned around expecting to see ye, but it was no ye, it was the English lord."

Connor stiffened even more after she mentioned the English lord, his mind started to race with what possibly could have happened. *Did that filthy Englishman dishonor my Heather! If he did, I will cut his throat!* This thought outraged Connor, but instead of voicing his anger, he took a deep breath, and after he let it out, he brought his anger under control. Keeping his face neutral, *it will no matter. I will still marry her. Nothing she or what happened will change how I feel for her!* he thought.

Staring down at the ground, "Connor, something happened. My heart…there was something, a connection, one I no felt for anyone but ye. This man, this English lord, there was something familiar…" Heather stopped, she had to see how her words were affecting him, and when she looked up, at first, she didn't see anything that betrayed what he was feeling, and then she saw him standing rigid as if he was ready to attack, and in his eyes, she saw rage. Heather placed her hand on his arm, "Connor, he did no dishonor me, nor did I dishonor ye," she said, and immediately saw the tension, even if just a little, eased from his body.

Unbeknownst to Heather, Connor was soring with anger, although the tension lessened, there was nothing he could say except, "finish," through clenched teeth.

With that, Heather nodded and continued, "I felt as if I knew him. My heart recognized his, and apparently, his heart recognized mine. He reached for me, as I reached for him, and I allowed him to embrace me, as I embraced him. It felt right. We felt right."

Connor's heart sank to the pit of his stomach, unable to believe what he was hearing. *God, please tell me I am no going to lose her. I can no lose her. If tis to be, I am sorry to say, I will kill the man!*

"We both knew…felt it. I said, 'tis ye. I know, tis ye,' and he said the same to me. There were tears in both of our eyes, and for those few moments I wanted nothing more than to be with him," she said, turning away from Connor. After a few moments, she turned back, knowing he deserved more than the sight of her back, and she was surprised to see there was no change on Connor's face, but his eyes, said it all, he was angry.

Heather chose her next words with care. "I was prepared…to run away with him," she said, as she looked for a sign that gave away Connor's feelings, but still, there was nothing, and this scared her more than if he showed a reaction, so she went on. "My heart started beating fast, with fear of what my leaving would do to ye, and my heart sank. I pulled away and ran from him, but only made it halfway down the path, when I found the need to turn back. I had to explain to him, so I returned and told

Lord Booth I am to wed ye, and this can no be. I told him how much I loved ye, that my heart and soul belonged to ye, and only to ye. He agreed and told me he would leave at once and never return, even if he was ordered to do so. This was the last time I will ever see him, and he would tell the king… that Keith's land was no to be taken. This he could no promise, but he would do what he could to secure the safety of this land. He turned and walked away. After he left, I felt such shame, I could no bear to see ye, or anyone, and went to the only place I knew no one would be, in the cellar where ye found me."

Heather's last words shocked him, "ye been in the cellar all night?" he asked, shaking his head. "Lass, tis madness." At this, he couldn't help it, he needed her in his arms. "Heather, my love, no matter what happened, ye are mine. Do ye hear me? Ye chose me, and if ye did no…well, tis best I do no speak of it. Lass…Heather, I love ye. Nothing…no one will keep ye from me. Thank ye for choosing me. My heart could no bear to lose ye," Connor said, knowing he couldn't say what he wanted to say and do – he wanted to yell at her, to shake her, to toss her over his knee and spank her, but instead when all was done, he kissed her hard, and with more passion than he's ever shown her before.

Once they broke apart, Heather had to know, she had to ask him how he could be so accepting of what she told him. "Connor, how can ye not be angry with me? How can ye still want me? I betrayed ye. Maybe no fully, but I did, I betrayed ye."

Connor watched Heather as she spoke, there was so much love in her eyes, and he knew she could not miss the love he felt for her in his. *Ah, she does,* he thought.

With the way Connor was looking at her, she had to turn away from him, it was too much for her to bear.

Connor placed his fingers under her chin, and forced her to look at him, then waited until she made eye contact with him. "Heather, my love, do ye no realize how much I love ye? I know we have no known each other long, but ye are already a part of my heart and soul. There is nothing ye could do that would force me to turn away from ye. I know ye feel the same, or ye would no be here now standing before me. I own yer heart and soul as ye own mine."

Heather was shocked at Connor's declaration, at the same time, she was amazed by the man standing before her. He was right, he was already a part of her heart and soul. No, they haven't known each other long, but her heart and soul recognized his belonging to her. He was her Connor, her man, and soon, he would be her husband. Heather looked at him, deep into his eyes, and saw he spoke the truth. The love she saw left her weak in the knees, and from that moment, her heart was fully his.

Heather reached up and cupped Connor's face, "Connor," she said, looking directly into his eyes, "I love ye, more than I could ever say. Ye are my heart and soul. If I were to ever lose ye, I shall follow ye in death as I do in life."

For Connor to see the love Heather has for him in her eyes, sent his heart soaring with joy, but her last words stunned him, and this, this was something he could not allow. "No, ye will no follow me. No matter what, ye will no follow me." Before Heather could respond, Connor took her mouth with his, and all was forgotten.

Chapter 6

The following morning after morning meal, Connor took Heather to his – their favorite place, the cliff that overlooked the sea that also sat on the edge of the forest.

"Aye, tis no grand? Look, Connor, look at God's glorious beauty?" Heather said, with her arms stretched out to her sides as she took in the beauty of the place before her.

"Aye, my love, I am sure tis grand, but all I see before me is the beauty of a lass so bonny," he said, although the beauty was grand, the sight of this lass – his lass, was all he could see.

"Connor," she said, putting her hands on her hips, "do no be foolish. Come see," putting her hand out to him, "the beauty I see."

"Ah lass, come, let me wrap my arms around ye," Connor said as he took her hand and pulled her close to his body, "tis all I desire now," as he took Heather in his arms and into a loving embrace. After a few moments, he leaned down and kissed her with all the love and passion he had, and Heather accepted his offer, returning it with the same love and passion. "Ah lass," he said, breaking the kiss and resting his forehead against hers. "Ye are bonny, and I can no wait to make ye my wife. When our clans come together, all of this," looking up to the beauty before him – the highlands, "shall be yer's," he said with a smile.

"Connor —" was all she managed to say before he kissed her again.

On the following morning, Heather went to hers and Connor's favorite place, and while she was standing at the edge of the cliff looking out to the sea, with her hair flapping in the wind, as the strong sea breeze caressed her face, she suddenly heard footsteps approaching from behind, and when she turned around and saw Connor, she smiled as she started towards him, but he put his hand up to stop her.

When Connor first saw Heather, the look of her took his breath away, and when she turned to come to him, he stopped her, needing to cherish the way she looked as he slowly made his way to her, and when he finally made it to her side, he took a piece of hair that was blowing around her face and tucked it behind her ear, looking down at her with a tremendous amount of love.

"Aye, love, what are ye doing here? Do ye no get enough of this place?" he said with a smile.

"Ah, no my love, this place is so beautiful, I come here as much as I can, and to have ye here and share this with ye, tis brings me great joy and causes my heart to swell with love for ye. I never thought I could love ye as much as I do now. I can no wait for the day when we wed, and I am finally yer wife and ye are my husband."

"Aye love, nor can I. Nor can I," he whispered, finding it hard to speak with the love he feels for this woman.

Connor pulled Heather into an embrace, resting her head against his chest directly over his heart, and when Heather heard his heart race, she knew it was from the love he felt for her.

"Aye, my love, I love ye so much and soon I will be yer wife."

"Aye love, that ye will be. Come, love, we must return to the castle to meet with my and yer da.

"Nae Connor, I want to stay here for a little longer."

Connor smiled, "aye love, but no stay long aye."

Heather smiled, "aye Connor, I will no stay long."

With that, Connor kissed Heather, then turned and left to meet with his father and Laird Campbell to finalize their marriage contract.

After Connor left, Heather stood admiring the sea when she heard soft footsteps approaching, thinking it was Connor, she turned and was prepared to embrace him, but instead of Connor, it was an old woman, who appeared to be coming out of the mist, when only moments ago, there was none. *Mist, where did it come from,* she thought.

"Aye lass, what are ye doing alone in the cold?" the old woman asked in a scratchy voice.

The woman frightened Heather, and she quickly looked to see if Connor was in eyes view, but he was already out of sight. As she looked at this old woman, she didn't see there was anything to be afraid of, but then, why did her skin crawl at the sight of her?

The old woman was short in stature and was standing just at the edge of the forest tree line, appearing to be looking for something, maybe expecting someone else. Heather looked around, she was surprised to see someone outside of the Keith clan, a stranger, and she wondered how she managed to get passed the guards.

Who is this woman? Heather thought. Then, realizing she'd forgotten her manners, "good day to ye mistress. Tis a beautiful day, is it no? What are ye doing on Keith's land, and how did ye manage to get passed the guards?"

The old woman smiled, not deterred by Heather's words, "aye, so many questions. Tis so, but I had to come when I felt ye, and when I saw ye, I recognized who ye are. Ye are an old soul. One of us, ye are," she said.

"One of ye? What do ye mean? Are ye no Scottish? You speak as ye are Scottish."

"Aye, but no of yer time," she said, as she watched Heather carefully. First, she saw Heather's confusion, then, she saw shock, when she realized and with understanding who this woman might be, but she had to be sure.

Slowly and carefully, "time?" she asked, then took a moment before she asked her next question, "ye are no of this time? Nae, tis no possible."

"Go on child, ask what ye believe to be true."

Nae, tis no possible. "Ye…are Fae…are ye no?" she asked with surprise and wonder.

The old woman smiled, but she did not answer Heather, instead, she said, "ye are of the land, are ye no?"

Heather looked at the old woman with a questionable eye, not understanding what she meant. Before she had the chance to inquire, the old woman continued, "ye love the land and ye spend a great deal of yer time outdoors, do ye no?"

Again, Heather could only stare at the old woman, and when she finally found her voice she said, "aye, tis so. I would rather be outdoors than stuck between stone walls."

The old woman smiled, "aye lass, ye are the one. Ye shall see me again," the old woman said, then turned and disappeared into the forest beyond the mist, which appeared out of nowhere, leaving Heather standing alone stunned by what she witnessed.

After Heather returned to the castle she searched for Connor, and when she found him, she took him to the sitting room and told him about the strange encounter she had with the old woman.

"Connor, do ye believe in the Fae?" she asked.

"Aye, ye can no be Scottish without believing in the Fae."

"Connor, what if I tell ye I met a Fae?"

Connor stiffened and stared at Heather for a long moment before he asked, "love, what do ye mean, ye met a Fae?"

"Connor, after ye returned to the castle to talk with da and Laird Keith —"

Shaking his head, "nae, tis yer da now too. Ye must address him as so," he said giving her a sly smile.

Heather smiled, "after ye left, an old woman appeared and spoke with me. Connor, she is Fae, and she is from a different time. She said I am one of theirs, who is one with the land. I no understand what she means or why she sought me out, but I was no afraid of her. Well, at first, I was, but when I talked to her, I was no more. Instead, I felt protected."

As Connor was listing to Heather, he wasn't sure what to say. He believed what she said to be true, but can he truly believe she met a – Fae? Shaking his head no, but he believed and trusted Heather.

"Aye, is this so. Do ye no why she appeared to ye?" he asked, but without waiting for an answer he continued, "I can no understand why. I have heard if a Fae appears to ye, it can be a blessing or a curse. If ye did no feel bad, and ye felt protected, then I can only believe it is a blessing," he said with a smile.

"'Tis strange, I know. I no naught what to make of it."

"Aye love, nor do I, but we shall look at it as a blessing for our upcoming wedding," he said, then kissed her.

Later that evening while Connor and Heather were alone in the sitting room sharing stories about each other's lives.

"My mother died when I was but a lad. She is buried in the kirkyard. I try to see and speak to her every day, but since ye arrived I have no gone. Will ye…will ye come with me in the morning?" Connor asked.

While Heather listened to Connor speak of his mother, her heart ached for him, and she took his hand and held it in hers. "I am sorry Connor. I will be honored to go with ye to see yer mother. I too lost my mother when I was a lass after she gave birth to my brother," she said, choking on the word.

"Lass, ye need no speak of it if it is too painful."

"Nae, Connor. Ye shared with me, I need to share with ye," she said and smiled at him. "I love my mother very much and when she died, I was lost without her, but I took my brother and cared for him as she would have wanted me to. But then…" taking a deep breath, and after letting it out, "when he was but ten, I lost him too. 'Tis my fault it was."

Connor saw the anguish in Heather's eyes, and he immediately pulled her into his arms to comfort her. As she was sitting on his lap resting her head on his shoulders with her eyes closed, "we went riding and I wanted to race him across the meadow, and as we were racing, his horse hit a hole in the ground and sent Sean flying through the air and he hit his head on the rock killing him instantly, from what I was told, but I blamed myself for his death," she said as tears began to fall.

"'Tis was no yer fault," he said as realization hit him, "ah, tis why ye no come before we were to meet. Da told me of yer brother's death, a great tragedy that kept us from meeting. I wish I could have been there for ye."

At this, Heather smiled, "aye, tis true, but it was a reason to avoid ye, as I have been before," she said, then sadness struck her again, "I wish ye could have been there. It could have made it easier to bear if ye were there to hold me in yer arms as ye are now."

"Love, ye have me, and ye always will. I will never leave ye, as yer brother and mother left ye. I swear to ye love, ye will no lose me."

Raising her head and placing her hand on Connor's face, "nae Connor, ye can no promise such a thing. The English will be coming to take our lands and ye will be forced to fight. I know this, and I know I can no stop ye. Ye are a warrior —"

"And a good warrior, the best in the highlands. No man can beat me," he said with a grin.

Slapping his chest, "nae Connor, ye can no promise me that. No this, if ye are taken from me, I will follow ye."

Grabbing Heather by the shoulders, "nae, ye will no follow me. Ye will no die. Promise me, ye will live for us both."

Heather had her head down, "nae Connor, I can no promise ye."

Connor watched Heather for a long moment, and he knew he could not change her mind, so he did the best thing he could, "then promise me ye will no do anything until you have my body as confirmation of my death. Heather, if I still breathe, I will make it back to ye, even if I am a broken man. If I am killed and my body can no be returned to ye, then I will send my best and trusted man Gordon to inform ye I am dead. If it can no be he, then there will be another, but love, I promise ye, one way or another I will return to ye. You can no take yer life until ye have proof I am no more."

Heather remained quiet for a long time before she finally spoke, "Connor, I will promise ye, but I can no bear to see ye dead. It will destroy me. I could no bear it. I will do what I can, tis all I can promise ye."

Connor knew this was the best he was going to get – for now. He plans on not dying, not for a very long time. Then, he remembered the Fae, "love, no forget, ye had a visit from the Fae, a blessing before our wedding. With such blessing, I will no die. I will return to ye," he said with confidence.

Heather smiled, "aye, a blessing it was."

The following morning Connor took Heather to the kirkyard to meet his mother. "Mother, I bring ye, Heather. She is to be my wife," he said, then he turned to Heather, "Heather, this is my mother."

Heather curtsied, "tis a pleasure to me ye My Lady," she said, turning to look at Connor, "ye have a grand son, and I look forward to him being my husband and if God is willing, give ye yer first grandchild."

Connor smiled, "aye mother, she is a grand lady, and I can no wait to make her my wife." Turning back to his mother's grave, "ye would have liked her. I am sure ye would have," he said with sadness.

"Aye Connor, she can see ye, I believe this to be so," Heather said, then put her arms around Connor to comfort him when she saw tears in his eyes.

Chapter 7

It was the day before Connor and Heather's wedding – they were at their favorite place in a loving embrace. "Ah, Heather, I love ye with all my heart," Connor said, as he softly caressed Heather's face.

Heather leaned into his touch, "I love ye, Connor, with all my heart. My heart wants to burst with the love I feel for ye."

"Love, ye are to be my wife, and I yer husband, we are to be together from now and forever."

"Connor, ye are my heart, I never believed when we met, I could love ye as I do now.

"Ah love, I knew when I saw ye, ye would be my heart, my love, and the one I was to marry. When our marriage was arranged, I accepted I may never love ye, nor would ye love me, and when I saw ye, my heart sang for ye."

"Ah Connor, I can no say I felt as ye did, but I was delighted when I saw ye, and there was a feeling in my heart, but I could no explain what it was. To hear yer words…aye, it was as if my heart was calling to ye. Connor, how is this possible?"

"My love," he said, pulling her chin up until their eyes met, "I believe it was God's will for us to meet. He put us together, how else can we feel so much love for one another so quickly."

Heather smiled, knowing Connor was right, and it allowed her to embrace what she was feeling, and she was pleased God gave her a man who loved her with all his heart, and for her to love him, in the same way, was a miracle.

"Connor love, never from this day will I be away from ye. On the morrow, we will marry and become husband and wife, and from that day, I never want to be without ye. I love ye so much there are no words enough to express how I feel for ye."

Connor smiled, as his heart filled with more love for this woman standing before him than he believed was possible. "On the morrow, ye will be my wife and there will no be a day I will no be with ye," he said, as he took Heather in his arms and held her tight against his body, and when he felt her arms tighten around him, he let out a sigh with the love he felt for this woman – his woman. *Nae, tis my wife.*

"Ah, tis be they are ready. They shall succeed in their path and what their future holds. He will be a good and powerful laird, one that can bring peace to the land and the highlands. Heather, has a great future, no of this time, but of a future time…life. Tis, important they survive all the obstacles they are to face, or everything will be for naught," the Fae whispered as she smiled.

There was much work that needed to be done to ensure her highlands remain safe and protected.

"There is a great danger coming, one that can destroy the Highlands. If Connor is no ready, the highlands will be destroyed by the English. Her love will save him and keep him strong, forcing him to fight to stay alive. The future of the highlands depends on his survival," she whispered, as she stepped back into the tree line and disappeared into the growing mist, one, that was of her own creation.

It was the evening before the wedding, and Clan Keith and Clan Campbell were gathered in the finely decorated great hall that was covered with greenery and flowers everywhere, along with the blend of Campbell and Keith colors.

Escorted by her father, Heather was dressed in her finest gown of the richest Campbell colors and wore her mother's Scottish pearls. Her father also wore his best tartan kilt and sash with a white silk shirt along with the Campbell crest. When they entered the great hall, all eyes turned to them, and the hall erupted into a roar of cheers and approval.

When Connor saw Heather enter the great hall, he gasped at the sight of her beauty, in the way her curly long orange-red hair fell over her shoulders was exquisite against the Campbell colors, which caused his heart to slam into his chest. After a few moments, he regained his bearings and stood and moved to be by Heather's side.

"Good evening, Heather and Laird Campbell," he said, bowing to them, but was unable to take his eyes off Heather, as he reached to take her hand.

Heather suddenly felt shy when she saw Connor, how handsomely dressed he was in his formal Keith regalia, of green, blue, and black, along with his clan brooch. He wore his hair pulled back and tied at the nape of his neck. To see him, made her heart swell even more for the love she already felt for him.

Heather lowered her head and curtseyed as she reached and placed her hand in his. "Good evening, Connor," she said demurely.

Laird Campbell watched the interaction between Connor and his daughter, and he was pleased with what he saw. After a few moments, he cleared his throat and said, "good evening, Connor, I see yer father spared no expense in tonight's celebration."

"Aye, he wanted everything to be perfect for tonight. He did everything he knew my mother would have done if she were here."

"Aye, he's done a wonderful job, tis beautiful," Heather said with awe.

"Shall we go and join my father?" Connor asked.

With a smile, Heather allowed Connor to guide her to where his father was sitting at the place of honor that was situated at the front of the hall. Once they reached the laird's table, Laird Keith smiled at his son and Heather.

Once Heather and Connor took their seats, Laird Keith stood with his mug in hand, "Quiet!" he called out and the room immediately went quiet. "As ye know, we gather this evening to celebrate my son's upcoming wedding and a great alliance with Clan Campbell. It also pleases me to know that this will not only be a marriage of convenience, but a marriage of love," he said, turning to his son and Heather, as the hall erupted with a roar of approval.

"Tis a great day indeed. To Connor and Heather, may yer love only grow with time," Laird Keith said as he raised his glass, as did everyone else in the room, and drank to the couple, and the festivities began.

Once everyone had their fill of food and drink, well, maybe not drink, Laird Keith singled for the

music to begin and the servants pushed away the tables and chairs to open up the hall to dancing, and dancing they did until the wee hours of the morning when Connor finally took Heather and escorted her to her bedchambers.

"Love, until tomorrow, when ye will become my wife."

"Aye Connor, I can no wait to be yer wife."

With that, Connor kissed Heather, a long and lingering kiss before he released her and turned away before he did something he should not until they were married, leaving Heather breathless.

Later that evening, after Connor escorted Heather to her bedchambers to retire for the night, he found himself ambushed by his clansmen. They picked him up and carried him over their heads and took him to their own celebration at the tavern in Stonehaven, where they celebrated until the tavern closed, then continued their celebration at the castle brewery.

As the men were enjoying their drink, they began to jest with each other.

"Aye, Connor we know ye are the best swordsman amongst us, but ye can no beat me in hand-to-hand combat," said George, "I can put ye to the ground and make ye eat the dust beneath me boot."

"Aye, if so, why no ye put up yer hands and face me and prove who is best," said Fredrick.

"Aye, I could if ye were no full of drink. The fight would no be fair," said Dougal.

"Aye, ye think so, do ye," Connor said as he staggered towards Dougal with one hand raised in a fist, and with his other hand, he dumped his drink over Dougal's head, which caused all the men to roar with laughter.

It was the day of their wedding and Heather was a bundle of nerves. The night before, after the festivities, her father presented her with her mother's wedding gown. It was a surprise, as she didn't know her father had saved her mother's wedding gown all these years, and after a few alterations, since her mother was a great deal shorter and smaller in the waist than she was, it was a perfect fit.

The gown was beautiful – it was a cream color made of the finest silk that was bordered with French lace, and it flowed smoothly past her feet. She wore a sash of Clan Campbell colors along with Keith colors draped across the front of her gown. A symbol of two clans coming together as one. Heather's maid did up her hair in an intricate braid, and once she was done, she looked like a princess.

When Connor sees me, he will no be able to take his eyes off me, she thought.

"My lady, Lord Connor will nae be able to take his eyes off ye when he sees ye in tis gown," her maid said, standing back to admire her.

"Thank ye, Mary, I was just thinking the same thing, though I wonder how Connor will look in his formal clan dress."

"Aye, My Lady, I am sure he will look very handsome."

"Yes Mary, I am sure ye are right."

Just then, there was a knock on the door, and when Mary opened it, she found Laird Campbell on the other side dressed in his finest, ready to escort his daughter to the chapel.

"Heather are ye —" Lord Campbell stopped when he saw his daughter, the sight of her in her mother's gown took his breath away, an exact image of her mother when she wore the gown on his wedding day.

"Ah, lass, ye are just as beautiful as yer mother was on our wedding day."

Heather smiled, "thank ye, da, tis means a great deal to me that ye saved mother's gown for me to wear. I feel she is with me and happy I am wearing her gown. Thank ye, da," she said, rushing to her father and throwing her arms around him.

Lord Campbell pulled his daughter into an embrace, and after a few moments, he escorted her down the hall and the stairs and out the door until they were standing outside the chapel door.

"Daughter, ye are shaking like a leaf. There is no reason to be nervous," he said with a smile. "Are ye ready?"

Heather took a deep breath and after slowly releasing it, she said, "aye da, I am ready."

With that, Lord Campbell pushed open the doors and Heather received her first glimpse of the chapel. It was magnificent – draped with gold and white cloth mixed with the Keith and Campbell colors, a sign of two clans merging as one. There was greenery in a watery cascade flowing down the walls, and at the front of the chapel stood a table with white and gold coverings with a Keith banner across the middle. Sitting on top, were two gold candle holders with white tapered candles and two gold goblets. The isle from the door to the front of the chapel was made of white and gold silk, that was sprinkled with red rose peddles. It was breathtaking.

When Lord Campbell opened the door, Connor received his first glimpse of Heather, and the sight of her took his breath away, stunned by her beauty.

"Breathe Lad, or ye be dead before ye are married," said his best man Gordon, with a chuckle."

Heather took a deep breath as her father proceeded to guide her down the aisle to the man waiting for her, and once they approached the alter, her father smiled at Connor and placed her hand in his, then turned and took his seat.

Once Connor and Heather were standing face to face holding hands, they couldn't take their eyes off each other as the ceremony began.

"Today is a grand day, a day I marry my son, Connor, to this lovely lass Heather in marriage." Everyone cheered and roared with acceptance. "This is a grand merger between two great clans, the Campbells and the Keiths, uniting us as one," he said, receiving another round of cheers, then Laird Keith put his hand up to silence them.

"Connor and Heather, as we are gathered here to witness this union, a marriage of love, Heather with ye hand in Connor's," Laird Keith raised the Keith tartan in the air, "I place this cloth of Keith clan colors," he began, as he placed the cloth over their hands, wrapping it three times binding their hands together as he said, "I bind thee, Connor and Heather, so thy souls and hearts shall be one. I bind thee blood and bone, so thee become one. I bind thee to land and water, shall both ye be one. I bind thee Connor and Heather, Clan Campbell with Clan Keith, so we shall be one," he said, then nodded for Connor to say the oath.

"My blood, my body, my heart, and my soul, I give to ye, forever more."

Laird Keith nodded to Heather.

"My blood, my body, my heart, and my soul, I give to ye, forever more."

"With these words spoken, I bind these two people, who were once two, have now become one, husband and wife!" he yelled with excitement. "Well lad, what are ye waiting for, kiss yer bride."

Without further prompting, Connor grabbed Heather and kissed her, as everyone roared. Once done, the wedding celebration began. With his mouth close to Heather's ear he whispered, "I love ye wife, and I can no wait until we are alone."

Heather blushed, but Connor's words thrilled her, this man who was now her husband.

The celebration went on to the wee hours of the night before Connor finally took his bride to his bedchamber – their bedchambers. "Alone at last," he said, watching Heather under hooded eyes.

Heather suddenly felt nervous, and gave him a slight smile, before turning away from him to look at the room. "Tis yer bedchamber? Tis beautiful, with the candles and flowers filling the room," she said with amazement.

Connor smiled, he could see she was nervous about their first night together, so he said, "my love," placing his hands on her shoulders, "tis no reason to be nervous, I will be gentle with ye. Ye own my heart lass, and I only want to please ye and make ye happy."

Sighing, Heather turned and looked at Connor and smiled, "Connor, I no fear ye, my love. I —" she stopped as she was unsure what she wanted to say.

To make it easy for her, Connor leaned down and kissed her. With Heather being unable to resist him, she melted into his kiss and touch. She took from him what he offered with the same fierce and passion he gave her. Connor removed Heather's gown and shift and once she was naked, he stood back to admire the beauty before him, and after a few moments, he removed his tartan. Once he was standing in front of Heather naked, she couldn't help but admire his strong body, and when her eyes dropped to his groin, her eyes widen with surprise, and yet with admiration for what she saw. Before she could act, Connor swooped her up into his arms and carried her to the fur-covered bed where he gently laid her down.

Once Heather was lying on the bed, with candlelight dancing on her body, Connor said, "my love, ye are the most beautiful woman I have ever seen."

Heather smiled, "aye, how many other women have ye seen?" she said with amusement.

Connor tore his eyes away from her body to look at her face, and when he saw the amusement in her eyes, he said, "aye, no many." Then, without further words, Connor slowly and gently crawled on top of her, and once he was hovering over her body, he kissed her long and hard, at the same time, preparing her for his invasion, and once he eased himself into her core, he made passionate love to her. Showing Heather in every possible way how much he loved her, and it pleased him after a few moments when she relaxed and returned with the same passion and love, and they made love until the early morning hours.

After Connor and Heather made love, and since the room was dark, with the drapes covering the window, except for a few candles still burning in the room with enough light that allowed them to see each other's features. With Heather lying back against the bed and Connor laying across the foot of their bed rubbing circles up and down her legs. It was a perfect place to admire the beauty of her naked body, with the way it shined from their lovemaking, as their essence filled the room. They were the happiest they'd ever believed was possible.

"Love, ye have made me the happiest man alive."

Smiling, "and ye has made me the happiest of women."

When Heather saw Connor look at her with lust in his eyes, she knew what was coming, and before she knew it, he was crawling on top of her and pulling her legs until she was lying flat on her back, and he made love to her again and again, until they were both spent from their lovemaking.

Chapter 8

Several days later, Connor and Heather finally dragged themselves from their bedchamber and went to their favorite place, the cliff overlooking the sea. As Connor stood watching Heather spinning around filled with happiness, it took his breath away, and he sighed, with the love he felt for this woman.

"Heather love, come to me?"

Heather stopped, and when she looked at Connor, she thought, *mine,* and wondered how she could have been so daft, that she considered being with anyone else other than him.

With her heart filled with love, "Connor," she began to say, but before she could say another word, Connor was on her in a heartbeat, pulling her into his arms and kissing her.

When Connor released Heather, she quickly said what she had intended to say before he kissed her. "Connor, I love ye with all my heart. When ye look at me as ye do, my heart swells with love for ye. There are times when I think how —" Connor tried to stop her, but Heather put her hand up determined to have her say. "Nae Connor, let me have my say." Connor nodded and Heather continued, "how could I have thought of leaving ye. From the day ye found me in the cellar, yer love," lowering her head for a moment before raising it again, "shamed me. Yer acceptance made my heart soar, causing my love for ye to grow even more, replacing any doubt I had. When we married…our wedding night," she said, blushing at the memory, "was more than I ever hoped for. Ye love me Connor, tis I know, as I love ye, there is no doubt in my mind, my heart, and my soul. Ye are mine, as I am yer's," she said, reaching up to wrap her arms around his neck, forcing his head down so she could kiss him, and when she did, she poured everything she felt for Connor into that kiss, as he returned the kiss with the same fierce and passion, that neither of them ever imagined was possible.

An arranged marriage rarely turned into love, so for Connor and Heather to find love was a great miracle, one they would never forget, and would cherish every moment they were together.

Connor gently lowered Heather to the ground, where he made love to her the only way he knew how, by pouring his heart and soul into his lovemaking, merging their body and soul as one.

What can she say, her love for Connor grew to a love so powerful she couldn't believe her good fortune. As Heather lay in Connor's arms in the tall grass at the base of the forest trees with his arms wrapped around her, her heart was racing for the love she felt for him. Every time Heather was with Connor, brought her to tears for the way she felt for him. Their lovemaking wasn't just a physical act, but a way for them to express what words could not.

When Heather thought back to the time when her marriage was first arranged by her father and Laird Keith, how she did everything to avoid marrying Lord William, for as long as she could, but if she knew then that she would love the man with all her heart, she would never have delayed marrying Lord William – Connor. For her to find love with Connor, was a wonderful blessing from God, to have a man own her heart and soul as he did.

Thank be to God, she thought, then aloud, "thank ye husband for loving me," she said, choking on her words. "Never in my dreams did I believe to have such a love."

Connor stared into Heather's eyes for a long moment before he placed his hands to cup her face, "nor I love. Nor I," he said, then kissed her, allowing their love to transcend beyond belief.

It has been three months since Connor and Heather's wedding when they received word that the English has entered the highlands in their attempts to take the lands by force, and the man at the head of this invasion was none other than Lord William Booth.

"The man said he would no take our lands," said Connor to his father.

"Nae, he said he would do his best to no touch our lands. Ye know as I do, if his hands were forced, he would do what he was ordered to do."

"Aye, but I no believe he will do so."

"Let us hope ye are right."

Meanwhile, Heather was heading to the village of Stonehaven to do some shopping, escorted by Connor's most trusted man, his best friend Gordon.

"My Lady, how many more things are ye going to buy? I only have but two hands and arms," Gordon said as packages were piling up to his chin.

Heather smiled, "aye, I am done now. Will ye put them in the carriage? I want to go for a walk along the seashore."

"Aye but do no leave my sight. Once I put these in the carriage I will come and join ye."

"Aye, I will be fine," she said heading down the steps to the beach on the edge of the sea.

As Heather was walking along the edge of the sea, she turned to see where Gordon was, and he was just starting down the steps to join her when she saw a man come up behind him and hit him over the head. It was an English soldier.

"Gordon," she called out, but it was too late, he fell to the ground unmoving, and she began to head towards him, but someone grabbed her from behind.

"I do not think so. Ye will come with me," said the man in the redcoat.

"Nae, I must go to Gordon. Who are ye? Do ye no know who I am?"

"Yes. I know exactly who you are. You are the wife of Lord William the next laird of Dunnottar Castle."

With shock, not understanding what he was doing, "what do ye want with me?"

"You will be our prisoner and if Lord William wants you back alive, he will relinquish Dunnottar Castle and the surrounding land to the English king."

Heather was shocked, she couldn't believe what was happening. What would Connor do? Would he and his father give up Dunnottar Castle to rescue her? Nae, they can no do this. She can no allow it.

"Nae, ye will no use me to get our lands," she yelled, as she was fighting to break free from the English soldier, but he was too strong.

"I am afraid My Lady, you are not going anywhere except to see my captain."

The English soldier dragged Heather to his horse that was just a few feet away, and once he put her in the saddle, he climbed up behind her and grabbed the reins, then kicked his horse to get him moving. Heather could not believe what was happening, she squirmed and tried with all her strength to break free, but he was too strong, and as they rode away, she looked back at Dunnottar Castle and how Connor will feel when he learns she was taken by the English.

When Gordon came to, he had a large headache and sat up rubbing the back of his head, and when he realized what happened, he quickly jumped to his feet and looked for Heather, but she was nowhere to be found. Gordon quickly went to the tavern and asked if anyone saw what happened.

A drunk said, "aye, sshure izz did. Tis ash enslish soldsier who took yeshe."

"Shit, did ye see what direction they went?"

"Aayyee I done. Tis went thawt way," he said pointing south.

"Damn. Connor is no going to be happy."

Gordon quickly left the tavern and jumped in the carriage and raced back to Dunnottar Castle to tell Connor he failed to protect his wife.

Connor was in the great hall with his father discussing their plans on what they were going to do if the English came their way.

"If the English step foot in Stonehaven I will cut their throats," Connor said to his father.

"Connor —"

"Laird! Connor!" yelled Gordon.

"Here," Connor called out.

When Gordon entered the great hall breathless and agitated, Connor and Laird Keith became concerned. "What is it Gordon," Connor asked.

"Laird," looking at Laird Keith, "Connor," turning to Connor, "the English…they…they took," he tried to say, as he felt shame for failing at his duty washed over him, "they took her."

"They took who?" Laird Keith asked.

Gordon turned to Connor again, then turned away, "tis Heather they took," he said, turning back to face his friend, and he looked him square in the eye, "I failed ye. I did no save her. They hit me from behind. They no even gave me a chance to fight. When I woke, she…she was gone."

Connor was frantic at what he heard; at the same time, he couldn't believe what he was hearing. *No, it can no be possible.* Yet, to see Gordon and not Heather, he knew it was the truth.

"Those damn English soldiers! I will kill them!" Connor yelled.

"Son, we will no allow them to harm her. Gordon, do ye know which way they went?" Laird Keith asked.

"Aye, a drunk from the tavern saw the English soldier heading south."

Laird Keith turned to his son, "tis as we heard, they are camping in the south, just outside of Aberdeen."

"Aye. We will go at nightfall and destroy those filthy English fools!"

"Nae Connor. No time to engage in battle. Ye will go with Gordon alone and sneak into their camp and take her back when they are asleep."

"Da, I can no leave her in the English hands! She will be frightened!"

"There is no choice. If it is who I believe it is leading the English, then she will be safe and in good hands."

"Lord William Booth. Aye, he will no harm her, if he feels for her the way I believe he does," Connor said.

"Aye, tis true," said his father.

Chapter 9

Once night fell, Connor and Gordon rode out from Dunnottar Castle and headed south, the direction they believed the English took Heather. It took them only an hour before the English camp came into view.

"Gordon, go that way and I will go this way and we will circle the camp and take out any scouts and guards. But, if we can avoid them, tis best we do, so we will no be discovered before we have Heather."

"Aye Connor."

Gordon and Connor made their way to the edge of the camp without being seen or running into trouble. When they met again, they were behind the trees just outside the captain's tent, where they believe Heather was being held.

After Heather arrived at the English camp and was taken to the captain's tent, she was afraid but full of anger. Once they entered the tent and saw the man with his back towards her, "how dare ye bring me here! Ye have no right!" she yelled.

When William turned around at hearing a familiar voice, he was shocked to find Heather. "My Lady," he said with surprise, then turned to the man who brought her to him, "what have you done…you took Laird Keith's daughter-in-law and brought her here?" he asked the lieutenant.

The lieutenant stepped up proud of what he did, expecting to be well rewarded. "Yes sir, I brought this Scottish whore so you can use her to force Laird Keith to give up Dunnottar Castle and his land."

"You fool! I do not condone kidnapping!" William yelled.

"Sargent, take this corporal and lock him in his tent. I will deal with him later."

The lieutenant, now a corporal was shocked, "but…but…"

"Quiet! Take him out of my sight…now!"

Once the ex-lieutenant was out of Lord William's tent, he turned to Heather, "I am sorry. The…he did this without my knowledge. I made it clear there would be no kidnapping, raping, or killing women and children."

"How dare ye! How dare ye come to the highlands to try and force us off our land! Ye, ye are no the man I expected ye to be!" Heather yelled. She was outraged, and at the same time, hurt. This man she had a moment with, how could he do such a thing to bring harm to her and her people?

"Forgive me, My Lady," he said bowing, "to be amiss with my manners. I can get you a drink. Something to eat."

"Phish, no ye can no," she said with sass.

"Heath…My Lady, I did not mean for this to happen. As soon as it is light, I will personally take you back to Dunnottar Castle. You have my word as lord and as an English soldier."

For a long moment, Heather could only stare at the man, and after a few moments, she knew he had nothing to do with her being there. "I would be very grateful to ye. I must return before Con…William does something horrible."

"He will come after you. I know he will. It is what I would do as soon as I learned you were taken. We might meet him on our way back, but if he were to come here…well, let us hope I see him before my men do," he said turning away from Heather. "I am sorry about our last encounter. I heard you are married now." Turning back, "are you happy?

Heather was taken back by William's question, but allowed herself to relax, "aye, I am very happy indeed. William is the best man I have ever known. But, William, I…" what was she going to say. I have – had feelings for him. No, she could not say that. Whatever she felt that night on the cliff, was no longer a part of her. Connor owned her heart and soul now, and she belonged to no other man but him. "I am sorry for what happened. It was wrong…and I am sorry," she said looking down at the ground.

William started towards Heather with the need to comfort her, but then stopped. "There is no need to be sorry. It was not your fault. I was the one to blame. Will you forgive me?"

Heather looked up and smiled at William, and he almost fell over, with what that smile meant to him. "Ye are forgiven. If ye forgive me as well."

With excitement, "yes, but of course I forgive you. Please…please come and sit and allow me to get you some food and drink. You must be hungry and thirsty after your long journey."

"Aye, I am hungry and thirsty, and I accept yer offer of food and drink."

William called out to the guard standing outside the tent and ordered him to bring them some food.

Connor and Gordon were just outside the captain's tent about to attack the guard standing duty outside the entrance when to their luck, the guard left his post. Connor turned to Gordon, and both smiled at their good fortune. Once the guard was out of sight, they slipped from their hiding place and entered the tent with their swords drawn.

When Lord Booth saw William enter his tent, he should have been surprised, but he wasn't. "She is safe. No harm has come to her. You have my word."

"Ye had no right taking my wife from her home," Connor said.

When Heather heard Connor's voice, she turned and ran into his waiting arms. "Connor, ye came for me."

"Aye love, of course, I did," he said, holding Heather tight to him.

"Did he hurt ye?"

"Nae Con…William," she said, with a short turn of her eyes to where William was standing, forgetting she had to call him William when they were out in public.

Connor smiled, "tis alright love."

Heather looked up at Connor, "he did no hurt me. It was no his idea to take me, but his soldier, which he has punished him for going against his command."

"I made a promise to her and your clan, I would do what I can to protect you and your land, but that promise is becoming harder to keep," he said with shame.

"Ye showed to be an honorable man, and if ye said ye did no plan this, I believe ye, but I will be taking my wife and returning to Dunnottar Castle."

"I or my men will not stop you," William said, and just then the guard entered the tent and drew his sword. "Put your sword away. These people are here as my guest and they will leave as such," he said in an authoritative voice, one that was not to be questioned.

"As you wish My Lord," the sergeant said as he bowed to William.

"Lord William, you are free to go in peace with your wife. No harm will come to you. Sergeant, make sure they are seen safely past the guards and are not touched."

Bowing, "as you wish My Lord."

"Safe travels, and it was nice seeing you again Lady Heather. I wish you well and much happiness with your marriage," William said as he bowed.

"Thank you, Lord William. I can no say I look forward to our next meeting."

"Until we meet again. Good evening," William said, then turned his back on them, unable to watch Heather leave.

Connor, Gordon, and Heather followed the guard who led them out of the camp and past the guards and scouts hiding in the forest until they were beyond the camp, then made their way to where they had secured their horses and headed home.

As William watched Heather leave, he felt that part of his heart that was filled when she was in his presence, was gone once again.

I should feel shame for feeling as I do about her, but I do not. God help me, I do not, he thought, then thought back to that day he returned to the lake and finally dug the area he had that strange feeling at and was surprised at what he found, a silver bracelet and a man's ring with a gold stone with the Davenport insignia wrapped in a cloth, and once he held them in his hand, he knew what they were. Sighing, William turned back to his desk and went back to work planning his strategy for when they march on Edinburgh on the fourth night.

Chapter 10

Once they arrived back at Dunnottar Castle everyone was pleased Heather had returned unharmed. Once Heather left the great hall to her bedchamber to clean and dress, Connor informed his father of everything that happened.

"Tis good news, tis Lord William who was in charge. If was another, do no know if it would have gone so well."

"Aye da, tis true. I can no guarantee he will no march to Dunnottar, but I believe he will try."

"Aye, I believe ye are right."

It was a couple of days later when Laird Keith received word that William's men turned west towards Edinburgh. They were safe at the moment, but they knew that would not last long. For now, they and their people were safe.

For the next few years Laird Keith managed to avoid conflict with the English, thanks to what he believed was Lord Williams doing, but their neighbors didn't fair as well, and to help them, Clan Keith and Clan Campbell, along with every neighboring clan went to help their neighbors the best they could and managed to keep the English from taking their lands and for a short while, managed to live in peace.

For Connor and Heather, once the battles were over, they had the most amazing life together. Although they hadn't yet had children, they were the happiest anyone could ever imagine. Laird Keith was ecstatic his son found love, a love he too found when he married his wife. He didn't see anything ever coming between Connor and Heather, except for the rising news that the English were once again coming to Scotland, in their attempt to take control of the highlands, by once again attempting to overthrow the lairds who held them. A call to the clan lairds went out to gather so they could form a plan to fend off the English and force them back to England where they belonged.

The lairds were gathered in the war room at Dunnottar Castle to discuss their plans to prevent the English from evading Scotland – again.

"Are we sure the English are riding to invade Duart Castle of clan MacLean on the Isle of Mull?" Laird Keith asked.

"Aye, tis true. One of my scouts returned after overhearing a few English soldiers talking in a pub in Glasgow, on how the English were marching from England to the Isle of Mull to destroy the clan MacLean, which we will be the first on their journey to the highlands," said Laird MacLean.

"Tis no make sense. Duart Castle is no on the way to the highlands. Tis out of the way," said Laird Keith.

"Aye, tis so. Could it be Lord William's way to avoid coming to us?" Connor asked.

"Aye, if so…no matter, we need to stop them before they make it to the Island," said Laird Keith.

"Agreed. If we are going to stop them, we have no time to waste. Duart Castle is a long way from here, and we need to gather enough men before we can march and stop them," Connor said.

All the men roared in agreement but were hushed by Laird Keith.

"Agreed, we need to march and stop the English before they reach the island, but do we know how much time we have? Where are the soldiers? Have they already entered Scottish soil? We need these questions answered before we march into battle," said Laird Keith.

All the lairds agreed and decided to send scouts from each clan in search of the English soldiers and report back with what they found.

"There is no time to waste. They leave at first light, and we need them to return in five days to report what they discovered," said Laird Campbell.

"Aye, and let's hope when they find them, they are no close to MacLean land," said Laird Keith.

The next morning a scout from each clan paired up in two and headed in three directions in search of the English.

It had been two days when the first two scouts came across the English, five miles outside of the Scottish border.

"Aye, James, there they are?" William said, from Clan MacLean pointing in the direction of the English camping in the forest.

"You go that way, and I will go this way and we will sneak up on them and see what we can hear," said James, from Clan Campbell.

"Aye, but we need to get passed their scouts. Look, there is one there sitting in the tree," William said pointing at the English soldier fifty yards from where they were standing.

"Aye," said James, and they moved quietly through the forest blending in with their surroundings avoiding all the scouts they came across as they moved their way toward the camp.

Once they reached the perfect spot that allowed them to see and hear the English talking, they sat and listened.

"Those filthy Scots will die at the end of my sword," said one man.

"They will all die at the end of our swords. If not, we will blast them with the cannons as we did before."

All the men at the campfire and the ones nearby roared with acceptance.

When William and James heard this, they wanted to blast out of their hiding place and spear them through the heart. Instead, they held their place hoping to hear more information that they could take back to their lairds.

"Before you know it, John, you will have your way with those Scots in ten days hence."

That was it, that was the information they were looking for. William looked over to where he knew James was and with a nod, they both rose and headed back to where they left their horses.

"We need to ride with haste back to Dunnottar Castle and tell the lairds what we learned," said James.

"Aye. Let us move, and once we are out of hearing range, we will ride with haste, no stopping for anything."

Without further words, they did as they said, and when they returned to Dunnottar Castle in record time, they informed the lairds of what they discovered.

"Tis good news. Tis gives us time to get our men in place, either before or just as they arrive," said Laird Keith.

Looking to all the larids around them, "we will have all our men ready to ride in two-days time so we can make it before, or just as the English arrive," said Laird Campbell.

"I think we should travel at night while the English sleep and rest for a couple of hours after sunrise. In doing this, it will give us an advantage, in the hope we will reach the English in time," said Connor.

All the men looked at Connor, unsure if what he said was the right thing to do, then a man spoke, "aye, we can do this. We are highlander's and know the land better than the English. We have the advantage to be able to travel night and day, unlike the English," said Gordon, Connor's best man.

All the men yelled in agreement, and so it was done. In two days, they will leave for the Isle of Mull.

The day before they were to leave to meet the English, in what would be a great battle, Laird Keith received word that the English were informed of their plans to beat them to Duart Castle, and when he learned this, Laird Keith knew they had a spy amongst them. That evening, before Connor was to leave for battle on the following night, Laird Keith called for Connor to meet him in his bedchamber once everyone was to bed.

As they were sitting in the dark, in the far back corner of his chambers, Laird Keith said, "Connor, ye know where ye go is a trap."

"Aye, father, I am aware. Someone among us is a traitor."

Placing his hand on Connor's shoulder, Lord Keith said, "aye, Connor. I never thought in all my years one of our clans would betray us to the English."

"Aye, father, I know. I hope by going on this mission we will be able to flush out the traitor when he believes all is lost and runs to the English."

"My son, ye will be marching into a trap."

"Aye father, but I believe my plan to march at night and for most of the day, will give us an advantage. Highlanders only require a few hours of sleep, so while the English are traveling only during the day, I hope to reach them before they reach Duart Castle, if no then I hope we will arrive at the same time."

"Son, if ye were to die —"

"Father, I know —"

"What of Heather, she will be devastated."

"Father," Connor said, turning to look his father in the eyes, "tell none of this to Heather. If she believes I am walking to my death she will —"

"Do no think such a thing, ye are strong and yer love for Heather is strong. No matter what ye will face, ye will find yer way back to her."

"Father, if word comes of my death, do no believe it to be true, no until ye see my body, proof of my death…watch over Heather. I am afraid —"

"No need to worry son, she will be safe with me."

"Thank ye, father."

Chapter 11

It was the night before Connor was to go to battle, he and Heather retired to their bedchamber early so he could spend his last hours making love to her. Connor knew if he were to die in battle, or was presumed dead, she would take her own life, and he needed this night to convince her, that no matter what she might hear, she was not to believe he was dead, not until she saw his dead body.

On this night, Connor needed to show Heather the power of his – their love, that it was stronger than death. He needed to show her that his love for her would keep him alive, and he would do anything – there was nothing that would keep him from returning to her. His love for Heather and her love for him would save him. He would hold this night close to his heart and deep in his soul, a reminder that no matter how bad the battle became, he must survive, so he could return to her – his Heather.

Once Connor and Heather were in their bedchamber, Connor bolted the door to ensure they would not be disturbed, and when he turned back to her, he took her in his arms and held her for a long time, and when he put her out to arm's length, to look at her and take in her beauty, printing it in his memory so it would hold him through battle.

"Heather my love, let me look at ye. I need to take in yer beauty and hold it with me from the moment I leave ye, through my travels and into battle, until I return to ye side again," Connor said, as he caressed Heather's face. "No matter how long we have been together, my heart continues to swell with the love I feel for ye. Heather love, ye are my heart and soul. Ye are the reason for my being."

Heather felt such power in his words, and it felt right. Her love for him, the way it felt to be in his arms, all was right in the world. It was a perfect and safe world. When Connor pulled away from their embrace, Heather's heart stopped at the sight of him, and when it started beating again, she could hardly breathe with the love she felt for this man before her. Her Connor, her husband, who was her heart and soul. If someone were to ask her before she met Connor, that she would love him with all her heart and soul, she would have said, *I ken naught, as I have no had anyone but da and my brother to love.* To love Connor as she did, filled her heart and soul with a love she never imagined, that if she were to lose him, she would not be able to continue.

When Connor said he wanted to take her in, to remember her, her heart practically stopped at the thought of it, and then the thought engulfed her with fear. If Connor were to die, there was no question, she would follow him and join him in death as she was with him in life.

Connor saw the fear in Heather's eyes, and without words, he took her mouth with his and kissed her, taking her away from this moment, and to a place of bliss, as if time itself stood still, and everything around them disappeared, leaving only the two of them.

When Connor finally broke the kiss, it left Heather feeling dazed, as if she and Connor just returned from another place, outside of their own time. A feeling she felt every time Connor kissed her.

When he kisses me, she sighs, *tis as if we leave this place to one, tis exists for only the two of us.*

Connor pulled Heather back into the comfort of his arms again, "Heather, my heart swells every time I am with ye. How can one man love someone as much as I love ye. I love ye more now than I did the first day I saw ye in the great hall."

"Connor," Heather said as she rested her head on his chest. "I feel as ye do, I never thought I could feel so much love for ye. Ye are my heart and soul, Connor. Where ye go, so shall I."

Connor stiffened at Heather's words, he knew what she meant, and he could not allow this. Connor pushed Heather away from him, so he could look directly into her eyes, "nae Heather. Ye must promise me here and now, ye will no do anything until ye see my dead body," Connor said, knowing he could not talk her out of it because he knew if she were to die, he too would join her. "If ye do no see my body, then believe I am alive and will return to ye. No matter what ye hear Heather, ye must promise me…the love I feel for ye, I will do all I can to return to ye. I will no fall, knowing ye are waiting for me. Ye must believe it to be so," Connor said with desperation in his voice.

"Connor my love, if ye promise me, no matter what, ye will survive and return to me, then I will no believe ye are dead until I see yer body. Know my love, to make me do so, will kill me," she said, clutching his shirt with her fist as she pulled aggressively on it. "No die, do ye hear me. Ye can no die," she said in a shaky voice with tears running down her face.

Connor kissed Heather without further words. He kissed her with all the love and passion he felt for her, and Heather gave back to him with the same passion, and together it left them both shaky on their feet.

When Connor finally pulled away, he said, "make love to me Heather and let me show ye how much I love ye, so when ye feel my love, ye will know I will return to ye. Will ye…will ye allow me to love ye all night, so there is no part of ye that is no a part of me. Love me, Heather, as I will love ye?" he asked.

Connor's words weakened Heather's legs and she held on to Connor tight to keep her from falling. "Kiss me Connor and do no stop until it is time for ye to leave our bed."

Connor did not wait to be asked again, he did as she demanded and made love to Heather, as he never made love to her before, and when the time came for him to leave, he knew he would leave with a part of her with him as he traveled into battle, until he was by her side once again, *and in our bed,* he thought with a smile.

Right before daybreak, not wanting to wake Heather, Connor quietly and slowly eased himself out of bed and out of Heather's arm that was draped over his chest, but before he could move, he turned to his side and spent a few moments watching her sleep, blessed to have her, his wife, a great beauty, to be by his side. *The Gods have truly blessed me…us,* he thought.

When Connor finally got out of bed, he went and splashed icy cold water on his face, and after drying off, he went to the window and looked out, winter was finally here with the snow on the ground. He knew to travel in these conditions would be hard but moving will warm his blood. Looking over his shoulder at Heather, he smiled, *and love will warm my heart,* he thought.

Once Connor was dressed, he went to stand at the other window, the one that looked out to the sea, since his chamber faced the edge of the hill, the sea was his backyard, as he was thinking about the days that were ahead of him – the battle, the love he felt for Heather, and the future it holds for them.

God, give me yer strength in this battle we are to face, and the strength we need so we may defeat our enemy. If tis no to be, then give me the strength to live so I may return to Heather, my beloved, he thought, and suddenly he felt a hand on his shoulder, and he placed his hand over hers, "my love, ye are awake," he said.

"Aye, my husband, I am. What worries ye?"

Without looking at Heather he said, "ah Heather, I think of ye and my love for ye. The time has come for me to leave ye, to travel into battle. I was speaking to God and asked that he bring me back to ye," he said, then turned and pulled Heather into his arms. "I love ye Heather with all my heart and soul. I promise ye, love, I will return to ye."

Heather tightened her arms around Connor, not wanting to let him go, but she knew there was no choice, she must, she must let him go. *God, protect Connor and bring him back to me.*

"Connor, I know tis time for ye to go. Know I love ye with all my heart and soul, and I will be here waiting for ye when ye return to me," she said, then looked up at him, "I know ye will. Ye will return to me alive and well."

Unable to resist, Connor bent down and kissed her, with such strength and fierceness he's never felt before, and when he pulled away to turn and leave, he couldn't resist, he pulled her back in his arms with the need to hold her, as he struggled to let her go, but he must. So, with reluctance, he released Heather, and without further words, he turned away from her, strapped on his sword and dagger and attached his tartan with Heather's help, and walked out the door, but unable to help himself, he turned for one more look at her, and again, he couldn't resist, he went to her and pulled her into his arms, and gave her a final kiss, then went out the door and shut it behind him.

With fear in her heart, Heather watched Connor leave, and until that moment she held herself together, wanting to be strong for him because she knew it was what he needed, but once the door closed, she ran and collapsed on her bed and cried until she fell asleep, holding the memory of their lovemaking close to her heart.

Chapter 12

Connor was at the head of clan Keith and clan Campbell leading his men into battle, but since he left Heather, he's thought of nothing else but completing his mission. He wants the battle to be over as quick as possible, so he could just as quickly return to Heather.

Winter in the Highlands could be the hardest to travel across the land in, especially if you were on foot, as most of the men were. However, like himself, there were leaders of their clan warriors who also rode on horseback and the best way to keep warm was to ride as close to each other as possible, knowing their enemy slept, and when the sun started to rise, they set up camp deep in the woods, hidden by the trees, until it was close to early afternoon, when they rose and began their march once again. In doing this, they would hope to catch their enemy before they reached Duart Castle.

The English were riding to invade Duart Castle of clan MacLean on the Isle of Mull, due to Clan Keith's alliance with Clan MacLean, when Connor's mother married his father, in their mutual need to protect Scotland from the English, they would fight and do all they could to rid themselves of the English.

When they arrived just outside of Duart Castle, the English were already upon them, "how is this possible?" Connor asked Gordon, who was the captain of the Keith guards. "How did the English beat us here?"

"I no understand," said Gordon. "The information we received…we should have arrived a day before them. So," pointing to the English army that was marching towards Duart castle, "how did they arrive before us?" said Gordon, with the same confusion.

"Well," turning back to make sure they were out of earshot from the rest of the men, "I did no tell ye, but da and I learned there was a spy in our mitts, and we were hoping to figure out who that was during the battle. The spy must have ridden out ahead to inform them we were coming. Do ye recall a man leaving camp this morning?"

Gordon thought of the men sitting up camp, and there was one particular man that he caught leaving camp. "Aye, there was one man I caught leaving camp, he said it was to gather wood for the fire."

With anger searing through Connor, "who Gordon, who was the man?"

"Aye, it was Dougal from Clan Campbell."

Connor's head spun around so quickly in Gordon's direction, "what, Campbell clan? Nae, tis could no be, but now is no the time. We will figure this out later." Connor turned his horse to face the men, "men, what say ye, shall we engage in battle and do our best to keep the English from reaching the keep," Connor roared, and the men roared back.

Gordon wasn't only his captain, but his friend as well, the man he trusted the most. Without further words, Connor gave the war cry, and his warriors rushed the English and were on top of them before they had time to act.

As the battle raged on, Connor found himself fighting four English soldiers at the same time. Connor was a fierce fighter, a true highland warrior, he moved like lightning, blocking the blows he received from all the men that were around him, a berserker against the English. Connor wasn't only fighting for himself, he was fighting for Heather as well, to ensure he kept his promise, to live and return to her.

Connor took down three of the four English, but the fourth was as strong and as fierce of a fighter as he was, and due to the recent rain and snow, the ground was soft and slick, causing Connor to lose his footing, and the English soldier did not hesitate at the advantage given to him, and made his strike, plunging his sword into the left side of Connor's stomach, but it didn't deter Connor, it only made him fight harder and faster than he did before, pushing away the pain and the thought of any wound. He would not allow this English to take him down and away from his beloved Heather.

Gordon saw Connor take a blow, and although he showed no sign it affected him, he knew it wouldn't be long before he was in trouble. Gordon quickly dispatched his opponent and started to make his way to Connor, dispatching any soldiers that got in his way. Gordon usually like taking his time with the English, by making them believe they had him, but then as soon as they thought they won, Gordon would change tactics and come at the English more aggressively until the English fell. Now was not the time to play with these fools, and once Gordon reached Connor he jumped in and took over the fight.

"Go! Ye are injured, it will no help Heather if ye die!" Gordon yelled as he blocked each blow he received from the English soldier.

"Nae, I am good!" Connor yelled back.

The English soldier was pleased with himself when he struck a blow to the highlander, and when he saw him falter, he knew he had him. But then the highlander came back fiercer than before, however, he knew in time the highlander would weaken from his wound, and then the English soldier would make his strike, giving the highlander his final blow.

As the English were about to make his fatal strike, out of know where, and to his shock and surprise, another highlander came to intervene, and while these two highlanders were arguing about whom would take him down, he knew this was his chance, and he did not wait to take advantage of the two men arguing, and took all his strength and power he possessed and fought with such fierce so he could dispatch the one he already injured, and then after, the one who decided to interfere. But to his horror, the first man left and left him fighting with the stronger opponent, one he felt he could not defeat.

"Go, Connor! Ye are injured," Gordon yelled, as he blocked another blow from the English. "Go and attend to yer wound! Ye know ye will no do Heather any good if ye died! Did ye naught tell me to make sure ye do no die."

In this, the argument between the two highlanders baffled the English, which caused him to slightly relax, however, this would prove to be his undoing.

"Keep yer promise to Heather and go, man!" Gordon yelled again, and then turned his attention and focus on the filthy English soldier before him.

Connor nodded and ran north to hide behind the tree lines, not wanting to continue to distract Gordon, and on his way, he dispatched any soldier that got in his way, and once he was safely hidden beneath the trees, he watched the battle ahead, cursing himself for allowing that disgusting English to get in a blow. Now, instead of leading the battle, he was forced to watch. However, if he found he was needed, he would rejoin the battle. In the meantime, Connor ripped off a piece of his tartan and wrapped it around his midsection to stop the bleeding.

As Connor watched from the sidelines, and when he saw that the battle was lost to them, he came from where he was hiding, and after making eye contact with his captain, he gave the signal to retreat.

However, when the English heard the signal for retreat, he was determined to kill the highlander he was fighting. His moment came when his opponent looked away, and that is when he made his strike, piercing the center of Gordon's stomach, plunging his sword deep, then twisting it back and forth before pulling out, then sliced him up and down to ensure this highlander would not survive his wounds.

When Connor saw this, he knew it was his fault, and without hesitation, he ran to his friend's aid. Once he was on top of them, he wasted no time in killing the English with one strike of his sword, which the English didn't see coming, and once the English was down, Connor grabbed Gordon and threw him over his shoulder and carried him off the battlefield and behind the tree line where he had been hiding. Once they were clear from the battle, Connor laid Gordon down on the ground to assess his injuries, and what he saw, he did not like. He knew the injury was a fatal one.

"My lord, tis my time. Ye will return to yer lady alive. Ye will keep yer promise to her. I have done my duty to ye and clan. I go to my death the way a warrior should, in battle protecting my lord and my friend."

"Nae Gordon, ye will no die. I forbid it!"

Gordon laughed and flinched from the sharp pain his laughter caused at the thought of Connor 'forbidding' him to die, he knew his words were fruitless. "Nae, no even ye can prevent my death," he said, as he coughed.

When Connor saw the blood come from Gordon's mouth, he knew the sword had pierced his lungs, and he knew there was nothing to be done – Gordon would die. "Gordon, ye will no die! Do ye hear me, man!" Connor knew there was nothing he could do, but to see his friend this way, knowing he was going to die, was too much for him to bare.

"Nae, ye can no prevent my death. Remember me…" more coughing… "and if ye like, ye can name yer first-born son after me when ye and that pretty wife of yers have bairns." Gordon laughed, then started coughing again and took his last breath, and then he was gone.

Connor punched the ground, he was angry that his friend was gone, but then whispered, "aye Gordon, that I shall. We will name my first-born son after ye." Connor took a few moments to mourn the man he called a friend when he heard a noise. Connor quickly jumped to his feet at the same time he grabbed his sword, but when he turned to face the threat, he dropped it when he saw it was one of his own men. However, it was more from weakness than relief since the wound in his side had left his sword arm weak.

When one of Connor's men appeared at his side, they were shocked at what they saw. "My Lord, ye live," the man said with surprise but was more shocked to see Gordon dead.

"Aye, Sean," Connor said, as he looked back at Gordon, then back to his friend, "Gordon gave his life for me and our clan. We must return him home."

"Aye, My Lord."

"Where are the other men, Sean? How many did we lose?"

"No way to tell. We lost many, and many scattered at the signal to retreat. Right now, we must get ye to safety."

Connor nodded, then wrapped Gordon in his tartan. "Where is Dougal?" Connor asked.

"I no naught. I saw him run when the call to retreat was made, but I no see what direction he went in."

"Aye, tis know, he is the one who informed the English of our plans."

Sean was shocked to hear this, "nae, tis no possible. Dougal is a good man."

"Nae, he his no a good man, but our enemy. If I no make it, make sure my father knows the truth,"

"Aye, of course, My Lord," he said shaking his head in disbelief.

With Sean and the other men, together they carried Gordon to a cave they knew of, so they could hide until it was safe for them to travel and return to Dunnottar Castle. First, they will try to retrieve all the fallen men, if the English hadn't already disposed of them.

"My lord, should I send word to your father that ye live and we will return as soon as it is safe?"

At that, Connor collapsed and lost consciousness, and when he woke, Sean was desperately calling his name. "Nae, no until I am sure I will live. Once ye know I will no die of my injuries, then ye shall send word. I will no cause Heather hope, only to shatter it if I died."

"Aye, if tis yer wish."

"Tis is," Connor said, then he passed out again.

The other men of Clan Keith and Clan Campbell ran in all directions and those who survived made it to safety and searched for their lord.

"Where is Lord Connor? Does he still live?" asked Dougal.

"Nae, I saw an English struck a fatal blow and he fell in battle," said Lyle, who was but a boy, but what he saw was not the truth. However, the other men accepted this as truth, and after retrieving the other men, they headed to safety, and once it was safe, they returned to Dunnottar Castle to inform Laird Keith of his son's death.

I must find a way to get word to the English that William Keith, the laird's son and heir is dead. This will please them, and I will be handsomely rewarded, Dougal thought.

Once the men made it to the cave, one of the men asked, "what of Duart Castle? They will fall."

"Aye, tis nothing we can do. We will hope they can hold their own. First and foremost, we must ensure Connor lives and returns to Dunnottar Castle."

"Aye," all said in agreement.

Chapter 13

When Heather heard the battle was over, her heart sank, fearing Connor was lost to her forever. *No! He promised he would return to me. I must trust in that.* Heather's thoughts were interrupted by a voice calling for her father.

"My Laird!" A voice called out.

Heather, along with Laird Keith rushed to the main hall where she heard, "what is it, Brian? What has happened?" her father asked calmly, but with a firm voice.

Dougal took a deep breath and said, "they have fallen! Only a few remain, and there was no sign of Connor!" Dougal heard a gasp, and when he looked towards the stairs, he saw Heather standing at the base. Not disturbed by this, he continued, "I believe him to be dead," he said, then lowered his head, although it appeared to be in shame, he was actually hiding a smile. After gathering his composure, he raised his head, "I failed him, and I have failed ye, My Laird."

Laird Keith was stunned to hear this news, and his heart broke at the thought of his only son being lost to him and to his people. Laird Keith heard footfalls of someone running, and when he turned to where Heather was standing, he saw her running towards the door and into the night. He thought of stopping her, but he was sure where she was going – to their favorite place on the cliff so she could grieve alone. Although he wanted to stop her, he decided to give her some time alone before going after her.

Arran, another clan member from the Campbell clan turned to see Heather run into the night, and was concerned for her safety, "should we go after her My Laird?"

Laird Keith shook his head, "nae, give her some time alone to grieve. Once I have all the details of what happened I will go to her."

"Aye, My Laird."

Heather ran out of the castle as fast as she could, unable to bear to hear the details of how Connor died. *No, not again, this can no happen again,* Heather was saying over and over again in her mind, not understanding why she was saying those words. She needed solace, and time to understand what happened. Once she reached the cliff, she looked around, remembering the happy and wonderful times she and Connor spent together, the place she realized how much she loved him and would always love him.

Earlier that day, Laird Campbell had taken men to the north when they heard English soldiers were heading to Inverness, so he was not able to be there for his daughter when she heard the news of Connor.

"How can I live without ye?" she whispered into the night sky. "I can no. I can no do it. My heart hurts from losing ye. First, my brother, and now ye. Ye, who is my heart and my reason for living, and now, ye too are gone. Taken from me forever."

Heather heard a noise, believing it was her father, she ignored the noise and moved closer to the edge of the cliff, then looked down to the harsh waves smashing against the rocks below, and after taking a deep breath, "we will be together again. I love ye, Connor, with all my heart. I keep my promise to join ye in death," she whispered, then she took her last step off the cliff, and as she was falling, she heard a voice that was not her fathers.

"Ye are wrong child, Connor is no dead," the old woman said, but she was too late, Heather was gone.

Heather wasn't sure what she heard as she was falling, then the world went black, and she was no more.

The old woman was shocked at what she just witnessed; how could she have been so late. This, she did not see coming, not even with all her powers. If she had, maybe she could have stopped her. Sighing, the old woman turned to leave, *but I will no allow Connor to perish. He must live,* the old woman thought as she entered the forest and vanished into the mist.

Rebecca – 2021

Rebecca's eyes popped open as she jerked upright, *what the hell was that? Again, I fell to my death. Why? Why again? And it was in a different time. I was a different person. I was a redhead woman from the highlands. What in God's name is happening to me? No, not again. This cannot be happening again,* she thought shaking her head.

But it was, it was happening again. Rebecca was beginning to relive another life, one that was after she lived as Elizabeth in the 1500s, and she was determined to find out why?

Because ye were my wife.

"What? Who…what is going on? I need to know."

Spiritual Realm

Connor was amazed at how Rebecca was able to hear him. *Should I speak to her again?* he wondered.

"No. You need to allow her more time to figure out what is happening, and once she has, then you can speak to her again. Remember, she has to come to remember you on her own," said Joseph.

"Aye, ye told me. Tis very difficult to hold my tongue when there is so much I want to say."

"We are aware, but you must allow Rebecca to remember who she was on her own."

"Aye. Aye. Joseph, ye been around Rebecca a long time, how soon do ye think it will take her to remember?" Connor asked, anxious for Rebecca to remember him so he can speak to her.

"I believe it won't be long. When she went through her first life memory as Elizabeth, it was very difficult for her. This time though, since she is aware of what to expect and she now has Jonee and us to talk to, I believe it won't be long. You must have patients," said Joseph.

"Aye, but it no easy Joseph."

Joseph placed his hand on Connor's shoulder, "patients, that she will remember you. In the meantime, we will continue sending her the signs to help her remember."

Without waiting, Rebecca jumped out of bed and grabbed her crystal necklace and her laptop so she could use the keys to communicate with her guides.

"What is happening to me?"

"You are reliving another life. Not only reliving it, but you will also be feeling what was felt then, as you did with Elizabeth," her guides spelled out.

Letting out a breath, "they did tell me it would happen again," she whispered. Returning to her guides, "I heard a male's voice. Is this someone I can trust, or a spirit messing with me?"

"It is the man from this past life you are starting to remember. You can trust him," her guides said, then a flash of a man standing in the dark wearing a green – with what looks to be a black striped plaided kilt with a white shirt untied at the top of the neck. He had long wavy brown hair, with a thin mustache like she has seen when she watched the three musketeers, and he was smiling at her.

"Is the man I am seeing in my mind him?"

"Yes," they said, then they were gone.

"Okay, thank you. Well, here we go again," she said sarcastically, and then put away the crystal and the laptop, crawled back into bed and went back to sleep.

It was a few days later when Rebecca heard these words, *I love ye, Connor. Ye are my heart and soul. I never believed I would find a love as I have with ye. No words are enough to express what I feel for ye.* "What am I going to do?" she said aloud, then realization hit her, "a name, a name," she said with excitement.

A few days later Rebecca had this need to pick up a book that had European castles she bought at a used bookstore, and as she was flipping through the pages, she was concentrating on the Scottish ones, when she came to a castle that gave her that feeling, one she'd become all too familiar with, filling her body with a sensation as if butterflies were moving throughout her entire body.

The name of the castle was Dunnottar Castle, which now sat in ruins and was located near Stonehaven, Scotland. With that information, Rebecca grabbed her computer and began to search the internet to see what she could find about the castle, and what she learned, was for hundreds of years the castle was held by the Clan Keith, and with this information she heard the name *Connor,* whisper in her mind. Rebecca immediately searched for a man named Connor Keith but came up with nothing. So, for the moment, she gave up and waited for another clue to whisper in her mind, as she knew from the past, it would happen.

Weeks later, after receiving bits and pieces of information – memories of this life in the Scottish Highlands, Rebecca finally saw the woman; she was a redhead of the brightest red and orange color with sea green eyes. The woman was standing on what looked to be a cliff that overlooked the sea. The woman's arms were stretched out to her sides with her head back spinning in a circle as if she was taking everything she was seeing in, and when she stopped, she looked at him – the man Rebecca believed was Connor, with a smile and a look with so much love, it nearly knocked Rebecca off her feet.

Then, Rebecca saw him – he was handsome, with long dark hair, and was wearing traditional Scottish garments. His kilt was green with black stripes and wore a white shirt with black boots that came just below his knees. He was watching the woman with the same love she felt for him.

"What is happening to me?" Rebecca whispered. "I am not only remembering the life…I am also feeling it as well, just as I did when I remembered my life as Elizabeth, and I don't know if I can go through this again." Then, in her mind's eye, she saw an image of a man standing in the garments, but instead of seeing him on a cliff, he was in a place of pitch darkness, but he didn't have dark hair, it was light brown with waves that went past his shoulders, and he had a thin mustache as they wore in the 1600s. "Could it be him, and was this the time he was from, the 1600s?"

Rebecca didn't waste time. She grabbed her computer and searched for the name Keith who was laird during the 1600s. She didn't search the castle records, but photos of the lairds that lived during that time, and when she came to the photo of William Keith, the sixth Earl Marischal, she knew she found the one she believed was Connor. *Why Connor, if his name was William,* she thought. For now, she let that thought go, as she knew in time, she would discover the truth.

When Connor returned from battle, injured but very much alive, the first thing he wanted to see was his wife, Heather. He searched for her as he was brought into the castle, expecting her to rush to be by his side, but she was nowhere to be found, so he called out to her, "Heather, I am home love! Where are ye lass!" Connor looked around, searching for Heather, expecting her to run to him and welcome him home, but there was no Heather, and for the first time he noticed all the sad faces but didn't understand why, since he was home safe, and people should be cheering for his return from battle. Connor turned to his father, who had been by his side since he arrived at Dunnottar Castle. "Da, where is Heather? Why is she no here to greet her husband?"

Larid Keith looked at his son, this wasn't the way he wanted to break the news to him, since he was still so weak, but he knew his son would not be at ease until he knew why Heather was nowhere to be found. So, he took a deep breath and after letting it out slowly, he braced himself for Connor's reaction. "Connor —"

Connor could see his father was struggling to tell him where his Heather was but didn't miss the hesitation in his da's voice. "What da, what is it? Ye must tell me now!" he said through clenched teeth.

"Connor, we thought ye were dead, and when Heather heard ye were killed," shaking his head, "she was heartbroken and kept to her bed for days," he knew what he was saying was a lie, but to tell Connor the truth when he was so injured, he was afraid it would kill him. So, instead of the truth, it was best to tell a lie, at least until he was stronger.

"Nae, father. Heather would no be in bed if she knew I was home. Where is my wife!" he demanded.

Laird Keith knew he had no choice, he had to tell Connor the truth. Sighing, "to lose ye…she could no bear it, so she went to the cliff and…son," Connor's father braced himself for what he knew what his son's reaction would be. "Son, she jumped off the cliff and took her own life."

Connor's mouth dropped open, shocked at what he heard, but he couldn't believe what he heard. It could not be true, it just couldn't. "No!" he yelled at the top of his lungs, shaking his head as he tried to get off the pallet that his men made to carry him on. He needed to find Heather and refute what his father said.

Nae, Heather can no be dead. No! Not after what I went through to survive…for her! No! As Connor struggled to get up, his men held him down, but as he was struggling, he was reopening his wounds. His men were able to restrain him and between clinch teeth, as he fought through the pain he said, "where is she!"

"Connor…I am sorry…she is gone son," his father said, placing a hand on his son's shoulder, but Connor brushed it off not wanting his father's comfort.

Devastated, Connor was screaming at the top of his lungs for Heather to come to him. Begging her to come to him, to prove to his father and him that what he said was a lie. Yelling for her to stop scaring him, but she never showed. Shattered, Connor lay there with his eyes closed as they carried him to his bedchambers, and once he was in his bed, he lay there waiting for death to take him so he could join his Heather.

As Laird Keith watched his son being carried up the stairs to his bedchamber, Sean was trying to get his attention.

"My Laird. My Laird, tis important I tell ye since Connor is unable to," Sean said.

"Aye, Sean, what news do ye have?"

"I am sorry My Laird, but I know Connor would wish me to tell ye, even though he can no do so himself," Sean said.

"Aye, let me hear what ye have to say then."

"No here. Can we go to yer cabinet?"

"Aye," and Laird Keith led the way to his cabinet, and once they were behind closed doors, Sean began to tell him what they learned about the spy.

"My Laird, we learned the spy is Dougal from Clan Campbell."

Laird Keith's head snapped around so fast, shocked at what he heard. "What ye say?"

"Aye Laird. We no know why, but he is the one who betrayed us."

Laird Keith was outraged. He swung open the door, "Alec, come at once!" he called.

It was only a few minutes before Alec entered the cabinet.

"Close the door." Once the door was closed, "Sean, tell Alec what ye just told me."

And Sean did. He told everything that happened from the first day they made camp, on how Gordon noticed Dougal leave camp and how the English arrived before they did, when based on the amount of time they were moving, they should have arrived first, if not at the same time.

"How can ye know Dougal betrayed ye? Tis him leaving camp is no proof," Laird Campbell said.

"Aye, tis true, but there is no way the English could have made it before us unless thee too was traveling day and night."

Laird Keith didn't know what to think about it. Does he believe them or give Dougal a chance to explain himself?

"Call Dougal in. I will speak to him," said Laird Keith.

Alec went out to find Dougal, but he was nowhere to be found, and when he returned, "Dougal can no be found. I asked the men, and they said they had no seen Dougal since that night.

I went to the stables and the boy said he came and had his horse saddled to leave, and the boy said he thought he heard Dougal say 'the English will pay handsomely."

Laird Keith could not believe what he heard. "The English? Nae, this can no be so. The boy must have misunderstood."

"Aye, tis possible, but we must know the truth. There is an English camp near Glasgow, and we should send someone to see if that is where he went," Alec said.

"Aye, but Alec, ye and Sean must be the ones to go."

"Aye, we shall go at first light."

Although they managed to tend to Connor's wounds and believed he would live, but to heal a broken heart, there was no remedy. For several days, Connor refused to take nourishment, and as he laid in bed, he wished he had died in battle, because if he had, instead of him being in bed wishing he was dead, he would be with his Heather, thus, he prayed death would take him.

"Nae, let me die. I have no reason for living," Connor whispered.

"Ah, ye will no die, no when I am here," the old woman said.

"Old woman leave me! There is nothing ye can do to prevent me from dying. Tis my wish. My Heather is gone, and there is no reason for me to live."

"Heather," shaking her head, "tis a terrible loss. If all is to be as it should, ye must live. If no for yerself, then for Heather."

"Woman, ye talk mad, now leave me and let me die in peace."

The old woman snapped her fingers, and Connor was asleep. "Nae Connor, ye must live," she said, then placed her hand over his wound, where a burst of light came from her hand and within a few short moments, Connor's wound was no more. "Nae Connor, ye shall live," she said again with a smile, then she was gone.

When Connor woke the next day, he was surprised on how well and strong he felt. He placed his hand where his wound was and was shocked to find it was no longer there, and when he looked down, to his surprise, the wound was completely gone, as if it had never existed, not even a scar remained. "Nae, tis no possible," he whispered, and yet it was.

Connor had no memory of the night before, except for him wanting to die, so he could join his beloved Heather. "Heather," he whispered, "nae…nae, I can no live without ye," he said, shaking his head, then he turned and buried his face in his pillow.

Just then, the door to his bedchamber opened, and in walked his father. "Son, ye are well?" he gently asked, at the same time noticing the healthy glow to his skin.

"Aye da, I live," Connor said with shame and disappointment in his voice.

Lord Keith heard this and quickly went to his son's bedside. He took Connor's hand in his, "son, I am sorry Heather is gone, but ye must live. Even God wants ye to live. Ye are here and alive."

"Aye da, I think ye right. My wound has healed," he said looking down at where his wound used to be.

Lord Keith followed Connor's eyes and raised his eyebrows at the place where Connor's wound used to be. "Tis a miracle. How is this possible." Lord Keith said with astonishment.

"No idea, but here I lay alive, healed, and whole once again," he said with sadness and disappointment.

"Son, do ye no see, ye are meant to live. Ye must honor God's gift and live. Live for yerself and Heather."

Connor's heart sank at hearing Heather's name. "Leave me da, let me rest," he said closing his eyes as he tried to forget the fate that was forced upon him.

Laird Keith watched his son for a few moments before he quietly left his bedchamber.

After Laird Keith left his son's bedchamber, he was heading down for his morning meal when he heard his name being called.

"My Laird," called Alec.

"Aye, what news do ye have?"

"No here. In yer cabinet."

Alec, Sean, and Laird Keith went to his cabinet and after the door was closed, "so tell me, Sean?"

"Tis true. Dougal is working for the English. When we arrived at their camp, we saw him wearing the English redcoat laughing about how he fooled Laird Keith and Laird Campbell."

"So, Campbell was no aware. Tis good. I was afraid he was involved, but that did no make sense, no with his daughter married to my son."

"Nae, Laird Campbell no have anything to do with it."

"Send word to all the lairds of what we learned and to be cautious of other traitors inside their clan. Alec, check and make sure we no have another spy."

"Aye My Laird, I will do so at once."

"Sean, Connor is no doing well. I am afraid he will let himself die from his wounds," *tis best no one knows his wounds have healed.* "And I no naught how to save him."

"Aye, he blames himself for no sending word he lived. He wanted to be sure he was no going to die first."

"Aye, tis why he wants to die, he believes he is to blame for her death."

"Aye. Only God now can save him."

"Aye, let us pray they do." *Aye, God has already saved him,* he thought.

Chapter 14

It's been seven long days since Connor fully recovered from his wounds and attempted to renew his duties as the eldest son. Although he learned where Heather was buried, he hasn't been able to bring himself to visit her grave, he just wasn't strong enough, not yet. His father informed him that he wanted to wait until their clan returned his body, so they could bury them together, but after a week of waiting, they couldn't wait any longer, so Heather was put to rest on the grounds at the back of the castle, near the guard's gate and where the water flowed out the grate and down to the ravine below.

Laird Keith didn't want this, he wanted her buried in the family cemetery, but without Connor by her side, he could not justify doing so, since she took her own life, and he knew this would destroy his son, but there was no choice. Laird Keith marked her burial place by planting Heather's favorite flower, the Scottish Rose.

When Laird Keith saw his son staring in the direction where Heather's grave is located, he went to his son. "Ye will visit her when ye are ready," his father said.

"Aye, I will, but no yet."

"Aye," his father said and just stood by his son's side for a few moments before turning and leaving his son to his thoughts.

It was thirty days when Connor finally gained the strength and courage to visit Heather's grave, and as he was standing over her grave, he was stricken with an overwhelming amount of grief, and the tears he'd been fighting, he finally allowed them to fall. After a few moments, he regained control of his emotions and wiped away his tears, then straightened his shoulders and stood straight. He took a deep breath, and after letting it out, "Heather, my love, tis my fault ye lie here," he said, choking on his words.

"I have thought many times to join ye, by jumping off the same cliff ye did, to my death. If so, would I join ye —"

"Although grief consumes us and tis painful, do no close ye heart and mind to thy truth. Grief is painful, aye, but it can also free ye."

Connor was not surprised to find the old woman, and he tried to interrupt her, but she put her hand up to stop him, "nae, ye will let me finish before ye speak," she said. "Grief overtakes our sensibilities, our heart, and our soul. Do no let it rule ye, let it go, Connor. Grief…do no let it be yer end, but a time of great sorrow." The old woman turned away from Connor to look at Heather's grave. "Grief can be crippling, do no allow it, let it go. Live, no only for yerself, but for the one ye loss. Detach yerself Connor and let yer Heather soar," she said, then turned back to Connor, and looked directly into his eyes, "allow the power of yer love to wash away any grief and guilt, and allow yerself to live, not only for yerself but for Heather as well. Although she is gone from this world, she lives on in the next, never far from yer heart." She saw Connor was about to speak, so she held up her hand again, "wait, hold on to that place where Heather resides in yer heart."

Once the old woman stopped speaking, Connor was lost, he didn't know what to say, but her words – he felt them deep in his heart and soul, and he wondered why. "Old woman, why ye here? Why speak these words to me? What purpose do ye have to heal my soul?"

The old woman smiled, "ah Connor, I have a great deal to gain from helping ye, but this I can no say to ye, no yet. Know, I am here to help ye both," she said, as she turned back to look at Heather's grave. "Ye must live for her, Connor. For ye both. Yer time is no done. For it to be again, ye must live."

Connor looked away for a moment, needing to take control of his emotions, as they were so close to the surface, and when he turned back to the old woman, she was gone. Connor spun in a circle looking everywhere for the old woman, but she was nowhere to be found, as if she vanished into thin air.

When Connor returned to the castle, he was ambushed by his father, "lad, ye can no do her any good to grieve as ye are. She loved ye, and she would no want ye to grieve for her as ye do."

Connor was angry, and he turned his head so fast to his father, "no she wouldna I would be dead! I should have died on that battlefield! I should have died from my wounds! I should have died once I learned she was dead! But, God will no let me die," he said with disappointment before he was fueled with anger once again, "no, she would no want me to grieve, she would want me to join her, and ye and God will no let me!" Connor yelled, then turned and marched away from his father.

"Ah lad, ye can no live this way," Laird Keith whispered, then turned to the sky and to God, "can ye no help him? He needs ye more than before."

"Ye have no reason to worry. He will survive and become the man and warrior ye wish him to be," said the old woman.

Surprised by the interruption, Laird Keith turned and saw an old woman standing with her hands clasped in front of her. "Who are ye? I no see ye before?"

"Aye, ye have no, but I have been here, always watching ye."

"Old woman, who are ye?"

The Fae looked at Laird Keith with her head tilted to the side, contemplating what to tell him. *Aye, maybe I can tell him.* "Are ye sure ye want the answer to yer question?"

Laird Keith looked at the old woman and wondered if he answered yes to her question, would he regret it? But something in him wants – *nae, needs to know.* "Aye, tell me?"

The Fae smiled, "I am of the old days, the days when we were strong and free. When we were welcomed by all. I am one of the land, the water, the air, and much more. I am what ye know to be…Fae," she said gently, expecting either a shock reaction, one of acceptance, or one of fear. *What will it be?* she thought.

Laird Keith was shocked, but yet, not too surprised. He has heard that the Fae has been involved with the way the highlands have come to be, but also no one could understand why they don't use their power to rid the highlands of the English.

"Ye come here…for what reason? Can ye no use yer power to rid the highlands of the English," he asked.

Sighing, she shook her head, "ye can no understand our position. We can no get involved with events of history. We can only try to stir ye in the right direction. Ye have free will, and we can no change that."

With anger, "then why are ye here? What do ye want with Clan Keith?"

"Ah, yer son is my reason for being here. It was yer daughter too, but," shaking her head, "I was too late to tell her that Connor was no dead. She jumped before I arrived. Tis a few moments sooner and…aye," the Fae said with sadness.

"Ye went to Heather to tell her Connor was no dead?" Laird Keith asked with surprise.

"Aye, they both have a destiny, and I wanted to make sure she no did something to harm herself but, I was too late. Yer son though, he still has a destiny…a future, tis why I saved him," the Fae said.

This surprised Laird Keith. What was he to say – "ye save Connor? Ye are the one that healed his wounds?"

She smiled, "aye, I did. He wanted to die, and I could no let him. I shouldna, but he has a great future he must live for."

"My Lady, I owe ye a great debt," Laird Keith said, bowing to the Fae.

"Nae, ye no owe me anything. Just watch Connor and help him find life again. He needs something to give him a reason for living."

"Aye, ye are right, but what can that be?"

"He needs a duty. Send him to Laird Campbell to inform him of his daughter's death, and the reason behind it."

"I already sent word to Laird Campbell about his daughter's death."

"Aye, but tis better Connor go in person. He can take something of Heather's to give him."

"Aye, he can. I will talk to him. Thank ye, Fae."

The Fae smiled, and then she was gone. Vanished right in front of Laird Keith leaving him with his mouth open with shock.

When Connor's father told him he needed to journey to Cowdar Castle to inform Heather's da she was dead, he could not believe this fell on him. He asked why they hadn't sent a message before. His father told him they did, but it was better to come from him and in person. So, he did as his father wished, he rode out and met with Laird Campbell and informed him of Heather's death. It was the hardest thing he has ever done, but his da was right, after Laird Campbell heard about what happened from him, was the best thing he did, and for him to give back Heather's mother's Scottish pearls was also the right thing to do.

Laird Campbell was gracious to Connor for coming to him in person and explaining what happened and why his daughter took her life. His daughter loved Connor so much she could not bear to be without him, and that knowledge, although difficult, warmed his heart to know his daughter had and felt a great love, and for Connor, his heart was broken and may never be the same again. Laird Campbell insisted, that no matter what Heather said, he had to live. He had to live to keep her memory alive if only for himself, to remember and hold on to her love – their love.

When Connor heard this, it gave him something else to think about, something he hadn't before – living to keep the memory of their rare love, a love only known to a small number of people. *Aye, I will live and keep her alive through me and my memories. Although painful, she is still with me…alive in my heart.*

"Aye, tis what ye should be," whispered the Fae.

Although Connor wanted to die, to take his life the same way Heather did, it was not to be, he lived, although he didn't understand why – he lived. However, who Connor once was, was no more. From that day forth, he lived a half-life.

Then, ten years later, Connor suffered another blow, when his father died, breaking his heart all over again. After mourning the loss of his father, a great laird, he did what was expected of him, he took the role left to him, as the new Laird of Dunnottar Castle and the village of Stonehaven, but he would do no more than what was necessary, at the same time, he hardened his heart even further, to never be the same again.

It was too much for him to live this half-life, so he turned to drinking, in his attempt to numb his pain, to lessen the loss of the one woman who had claimed and owned his heart. That night, before he left for battle, when she told him if he was killed she would join him, and to his horror, she kept her word. When Connor learned she took her life, he wished he had died that night, instead of being left alone, he would be with his beloved Heather. When he thought of his father, he knew his father would be ashamed of the man he'd become.

Why did she no wait until she saw my body? I told her no to believe me dead until she did. So why. Why did she no wait? This, Connor could not understand, and at times, he was angry with Heather for not doing what he asked. He was angry at Heather for leaving him stuck in a world to live a half-life, numb from any and all feelings of emotions. When he had the need, he sought solace from another woman, but there was nothing more, he was detached from anything other than his own release, and once that was done, he was gone.

When Connor thought back to that morning when he woke to find his wound healed, he was angry and lashed out at everyone and anyone who came near him. He yelled and screamed to the heavens, to why God would take her from him. But he knew, it wasn't God's fault, it was his fault. If he had sent word immediately to his father instead of waiting to know if he lived, but he didn't, he didn't want to give her hope, to only take it away if he died. This decision would haunt him forever, a regret he would suffer for the rest of his days, with each, and every day becoming harder and harder for him to bare, thus, causing him to drink more and more. No one, not even his clan, his family, or his father could change that. His father, would he be the man he became if his father was still alive? This he will never know. All was lost to him forever. A lonely existence without the people he loved, which included his best friend Gordon.

What Connor didn't know, was even if he sent word that he was alive, it would have been too late. Those furthest away from him returned to Dunnottar Castle believing he was dead. Although deep down he knew this, it didn't matter, he'd still blame himself, and he always would. Instead of him surviving a great wound after a great battle, he suffered the destruction of his heart and soul. William (Connor) Keith would never be the same again. He died that day when he returned home and learned of his beloved's death.

The fun friendly Connor was no more, and what remained was William Keith the Laird of Dunnottar, who through the years sought every battle he could, no matter the reason, he hoped that one of these many battles would finally, after all these years, take his life, allowing him to once again be with his Heather, but it wasn't to be. No matter how hard he fought to die in these battles, he would always succeed, which earned him the reputation of one of the greatest warriors in the highlands.

One day, Connor's clan tried to encourage him to marry again. "Connor, ye must marry. Ye need an heir. Without an heir, ye can lose yer land to the English King. Tis I know ye do no want that." But Connor had nothing to say and just ignored them until they finally gave up trying.

Every year on the night Heather took her life, along with the night he returned from battle, Connor would go to the cliff that use to be their favorite place, that was now a place of pain, and where he attempted to find solace, but each, and every time, it would fail. Instead, he would use this time and place to speak to Heather, with an insane type of hope, that maybe, just one time, she might speak to him.

"Heather, my love, why did ye do such a thing?" he asked this same question each time, halfway expecting her to answer, which of course never happened. Connor looked down to the sea and rocks below, "maybe I should join ye lass. I can no live this nonexistent life without ye," he said.

What Connor didn't know, was this night would be different.

Appearing out of the mist, and in a scratchy voice, "ye loved her very much, did ye no," the old woman said.

Connor spun around when he heard the old woman's voice, shocked to see her standing on the edge of the cliff, where just moments ago there was no one but himself. "Old woman, what are ye doing here? Ye will get yerself killed."

The old woman laughed, ignoring his question and concerns. "Yer heart is broken, aye, but it will no remain so," the old woman said.

For a few moments, Connor could only stare at the old woman, not understanding what she was referring to, and wondered, *who is this woman and what is she doing here on the cliff so late at night.* "Old woman, ye should no be here. Ye could fall to yer death."

The old woman laughed at Connor in a way it made him shiver. "Laird Keith, ye have nothing to worry about. I am no that easy to die. Ye loved yer Heather very much, did ye no?" she asked, but this time she phrased it as a question.

Connor turned away from the old woman to look out to the sea. "Aye, I did, very much. Tis my fault she is dead, and now, I must live as a half-man," he said, not understanding why he was explaining himself to a stranger. Or maybe because she was a stranger and doesn't know anything about him or does she? Quickly, Connor turned back to the old woman, "what business do ye have here old woman?"

The old woman smiled, when she last left Connor, she took with her the memory of her existence until the time he was ready for her to reveal herself to him again. "Ye will see her again," she said.

Crazy old woman, he thought, but instead said, "aye, ye are correct. When I die, I will see my Heather again."

The old woman's smile widened, "ye shall see her before then, but…know, when ye do, she will no look like the Heather ye remember. She will be…different. She will be from another time. She will come to ye if ye wish it to be," she said.

This old woman is mad! Connor thought. "Old woman, ye make no sense," he said shaking his head. "What ye say," shaking his head again, "nae, I will no see my Heather again until I die."

The old woman recited these words, words she recited to him before. "although grief consumes us, and at times tis painful, do no close yer heart and mind to the truth. Grief is painful, yes, but it can also free ye. Grief overtakes our rational thinking, our heart, and our soul, do no let it rule ye, let it go. Grief, do no let it be yer end, but a time of great sorrow. Grief can be crippling, do no allow it, let it go. Live, no only for yerself, but for the one ye loss. Detach yerself, let them soar, and allow the power of yer love to wash away any grief and guilt, and allow ye to live. No only for yerself alone, but for the one, although gone from this world, lives on in the next, never far from yer heart. Wait, and hold that place where she resides in yer heart," she said, then the old woman reached for Connor and laid her hand on his arm, and when she did, Connor felt a chill that ran from his arm straight to his bones. "Ye will see yer Heather again, this I promise ye," the old woman said, and then vanished into thin air.

Connor was shocked when the old woman disappeared right in front of him, but then he thought of her words, words he heard before – *tis the old woman who was at Heather's grave, the old woman who healed my wound. She is Fae. She is the one Heather met that day here on the cliff.*

"Old woman return to me! Tell me what ye know! Ye are Fae! Ye can return my Heather to me! OLD WOMAN RETURN NOW!" Connor screamed, demanding she return to him. But she didn't, and after a while, Connor turned and returned to the castle.

Chapter 15

It's been fifteen years since that night on the cliff when the old woman appeared to Connor from nowhere and disappeared into thin air directly in front of him as if she was never there. There wasn't a day, Connor didn't think of that night, remembering the old woman's words, *those words…they were powerful, but how could I do as she said, and let go of my pain.* He more than once wondered who the old woman was – was she who he believed her to be or was she something else? And when he remembered what Heather said, of the old woman she met who she believed was Fae – *aye, tis possible she is Fae. The one Heather met,* he thought, but then shook his head as if that idea was impossible, and felt it was mad to think of such a thing.

However, since that night on the cliff, after seeing the old woman, Connor found the need to look towards the east without understanding why, and every night he would find himself sitting in the chair near the window staring out to sea as he thought about Heather, and wondered why he was prevented from joining her when he desperately wanted to.

Then, one night, and every night after, he felt a hand brush his face, and he was sure it was Heather. To feel her touch didn't frighten him, instead, it brought him solace, so every time he felt her touch, he would close his eyes and lean into the feel of her touch. But on this one particular night, it would be different. He didn't only feel her touch, she spoke to him, with words he did not expect. *Do no mourn me, love, for I still live. Nae, no in yer time, but in another time far in the future. Yer pain brings me here to ye.* Then, to Connor's shock, her voice changed, to one he did not recognize. *Our hearts are still connected, and when you hurt and grieve as you do, you call to my soul, and I find myself here by your side. I love you, Connor. Death, nor time can change that. If we have a chance to be together in my time, which is your future, then you must live and you must find love again.*

Connor was stunned, he didn't know what to say or do at hearing her words, but found himself holding on to every word she said, cherishing them, along with the feel of her hand on his face. Then, he felt a small breeze and she was gone. Connor slumped in his chair and put his face in his hands, "why does this happen?" he whispered, "it only hurts more when she leaves me."

After a short time, Connor rose from his chair, and with one last time, he looked out the window to the sea, then turned and walked to his bed, and after he lay down, he allowed himself to succumb to sleep.

The old woman's voice whispered in his ear, "aye, ye are a fool if ye no see the gift ye been given. Open yer eyes and yer heart and see what ye have." With a breeze, she disappeared as her words carried into Connor's dream.

While Connor was in a deep sleep, he dreamed of a place he didn't recognize, one, he was sure was not of his time, and when he saw a woman with long wavy dark brown hair, at first he didn't know who she was, but the closer he looked, he couldn't believe it, he recognized the woman – *Heather, tis my Heather, but no Heather,* he thought.

Seeing this woman confused Connor, and he didn't know what to make of it. With resistance, he pulled his eyes away from her and looked around to see if he could figure out where he was, but it was not a place that was familiar to him. As he looked around, he found he was in a large building that was made of glass, a structure so unfamiliar to him, he knew he was somewhere out of his time.

Connor turned his attention back to the woman he believed was Heather. She was sitting at a large table that appeared to be in the center of the room, and she was talking to a man with brown skin, and on the table directly in front of her was a strange device. *What is that,* he wondered, and before he could investigate further, he was awakened by a knock on his bedchamber door. When he woke, he felt confused and unsure of where he was.

<u>Rebecca – Arizona 2021</u>

You are my greatest love, she said rubbing her hand across Connor's face. "I've chosen you and I always will. It doesn't matter the time we are in, I will always choose you. Live my love, live for me, live for us. I need you in this time more than I've ever needed you or anyone before. So, live my love, live," she said as she leaned down to brush a kiss along Connor's lips.

"Damn, again I have a dream about this man…highlander, telling him I love him and I need him. Why? What does this all mean?"

Rebecca's continuous dreams about this highlander were beginning to drive her crazy. It's nothing like it was with Marco, no, nothing at all the same. With this man, this highlander, she felt – she had feelings for this man. She believed – she loved him. Thus, why she feels mad. Yes, of course, she had a feeling about Marco, but what she is feeling for this highlander went deeper than what she felt for Marco.

"I need help, and there is only one person who can help me. I must see Jonee."

<u>Connor</u>

Since he first felt her – Heather, every night in his bedchamber, Connor sat in the chair near the window looking out to sea as he thought of her, and when he drifted off to sleep, it wasn't a deep sleep, but a semiconscious one. This was when he heard her voice and felt her brush her lips against his, which caused a sharp sting, jerking him awake. He looked around half expecting to see 'her'.

"What was that?" he whispered with confusion, as he touched his fingers to his lips, but then after a few moments, he shook away the feeling as he stood, then went to bed.

<u>Rebecca 2016 Arizona</u>

Rebecca couldn't believe she found herself in another situation of dreaming of a man she had feelings for. Not just any man, but a dead man who lived in the 1600s. It was strange, since she believed by then she would be in a relationship with Marco, but instead, she found herself alone and once again having dreams about a man from a different time.

Although it frustrated Rebecca, she couldn't get the experiences out of her mind that she had with this man, this highlander, so she continued her search, trying to find any information she could, as she received bits and pieces of this Scottish life. She believed her name was Heather from the Campbell clan, and she remembered a brother who died when she was young, and she knew there was much more for her to learn. The only way to know for sure of what she was remembering was correct, she needed to travel to Scotland and to Dunnottar Castle. What it would tell her, she didn't know, and where it would take her from the path she was already on, that again was a question she didn't know. However, if it was anything like she felt when she visited Dunham Massey Castle, then she knew she was in for one hell of a powerful memory, one, she wasn't sure she was ready to go through – again.

As Rebecca was contemplating what she was going to do, she couldn't help but wonder, "seriously, what did I do to deserve this! I don't want to be alone, but what else am I to do? I have feelings for a man who exists and is alive in my time, but far out of my reach, and now, I am having feelings for another man in another time, again far out of my reach. Why? Can you just tell me why? What does this have to do with my life path?"

Rebecca became extremely upset, and at times she felt as if she was being played – something or someone was taking advantage of a lonely woman. Then again, she knew this was not true. After all, she was told that other past lives she lived would surface, but she believed when they did, she would have the support and love of Marco by her side, but instead, she was on her own and felt this new love was stronger than what she ever felt for Marco.

Rebecca went to Jonee, the psychic medium she found in 2014, but all she could tell her was, *yes, it is a new memory of a past life. If you need information, he will be the one to provide it. You only have to ask.* At first, Rebecca wanted to ask more questions, but then thought better of it – did she want to drag herself through another life memory that involved strong emotional feelings?

When this happened before, when Rebecca remembered her past life she had with Marco, and the connection they had, although it came to nothing, in a way it was healing. Rebecca forgave herself for the wrong she did in her past life as Elizabeth, and Elizabeth's father, mother, and brother forgave her. It not only healed her body but her soul as well. In doing this, she freed herself from the karma she created from her actions in that life. For Marco, now that was another story. Since Marco's grandmother Maria passed away in 2015, he became further lost than he was before, choosing a different path than the one he was destined for. A choice that would change the lives of everyone around them.

Seventeenth Century Scotland – Dunnottar Castle

It's been ten years since he had his first dream of this woman from, what he believed was the future, along with some type of experience from this woman – Heather – as if she was visiting him in spirit. He tried to stop the dreams by drinking himself to where he would pass out, but it didn't work – the dreams did not stop. He decided that maybe a change of location would do him good, so when he received a letter from the king of France asking him to visit him in France to discuss his efforts to remove the English from Scotland for good, Connor, without haste, he sent his acceptance and with a matter of days, he traveled to France.

Once Connor was in France, all his dreams with this woman, whom he believed was Heather, had ceased. At first, he was pleased, but after a time, he began to miss his dreams and the experiences he had with this woman. It was like losing Heather all over again, but he found the times he spent in France and with the king, he didn't think of Heather as much as he did when he was back home at Dunnottar.

However, he made the mistake of noticing one particular woman. While they were at the French court one of the queen's ladies in waiting – her beauty captivated him. At the time, his thought was only to bed her, but instead, since he noticed her in front of the king, shortly after, he found himself married, a marriage he didn't plan, nor desired since he never planned to marry ever again.

Connor was with his new young wife who was twenty years his junior and a real beauty, and he couldn't help thinking back to that night —

"Ah, my friend, she is a beauty. If you like her, then my friend, she shall be yours," said King Louis the XIV, as he waved for the woman to come forth.

"My dear, this is Lord Keith, he is the Laird of Dunnottar Castle in Stonehaven, Scotland. Make sure you treat him like a king."

The woman curtsied to Connor, "My Lord, it is a pleasure to meet you," she said in her soft French accent.

"Lord William, this is Sophia. She will take very," he said with a wink, "very good care of you."

"Your Majesty, I am honored, but I no need company this evening."

"Posh, she is yours. To not accept will be an insult."

Connor knew with this, he had no choice, so he bowed and took Sophia's hand, "tis will be an honor, Lady Sophia," he said bowing.

A Highlander's Love

Who would think, that one night with this lass, would turn into me marrying her, shaking his head. *Of course, the king gave me no choice,* he thought sighing.

It had been several years since Connor lost his one true love when she took her own life because she believed he was dead, so when the French king offered this beautiful woman to him – yes, he hesitated, but then decided what could it hurt if he took her. After all, Connor's been alone for a long time, and if he had to admit it, he was lonely, and to him, this woman was life, a life he stopped believing in. No, she wasn't Heather, nor would she ever be, but she was life to him, and there was something in him that said, it was time to live and love again. Can he, can he truly love again? No, he didn't think so, but he could try and live life again.

One night, a few days later, as Connor was with his new young wife in her bedchamber, he blacked out, and when he returned, she was saying, "you have never kissed me like that before," with her fingers on her lips, stunned by the shocking display of feeling he put in that kiss, and she wanted to savor the feeling, wanting him to do it again.

Connor blinked, he didn't understand what happened, but when he was kissing his wife he felt her – Heather, his true wife. Without saying a word, Connor removed himself from the bed and went to stand in front of the mirror to look at himself, needing to figure out what just happened.

He felt her, his Heather, this he was sure of. *How can this be? Did she no go to heaven? Her soul was pure…she had a good heart. Aye, she took her own life, tis from grief. She was no in her right mind.* Then a horrible thought hit him, *is she trapped here…God, if tis so, she can see what I am doing…betraying her and our love.* Connor shook his head, *no fool, tis no possible.*

As Connor was looking into the mirror, he could see Sophia, his wife. She was still on the bed sitting on her knees, and appeared to be speaking to him, but he heard nothing, but then, "why had you not kissed me like that before?" she asked, with her fingers still touching her lips where he kissed her, still savoring the feel of his passionate kiss.

With love, he thought. But that thought startled him and he shook his head, *no! No love! Never love!* The only woman he had ever kissed with such love and passion was Heather, his first and only wife, the keeper of his heart. *Tis possible, she is here? I felt her. I know I did. Tis why I kissed Sophia so?* He again shook his head with the need to rid himself of the idea. *Never again!* Connor looked up and into the mirror, to the woman kneeling on the bed behind him, then turned, and in a cold and heartless voice, "get dressed," he said and left Sophia's bedchamber.

<u>Arizona – March 2017</u>

Since Rebecca's first experience in reliving a past life when she lived in the Scottish Highlands, every day she saw things that reminded her of the highlands: a sign she never noticed before, although she's driven this same route for years, was a sign that said Highland Road. Another time when she was heading home, she saw an X in the sky directly over her house, and the first thing that came to her mind was Scotland. There were many more and when she watched a show with a Scottish song, the feeling she had was of a strong and powerful love, one she hadn't felt before, not even with Robert, the man who was her husband in her life from the 1500s.

What did all this mean? She believed Marco was her love, the one she was connected to and the one her soul was tied to. So, what did all of this mean? Was this the confirmation she was looking for, that she was tied to Scotland and this man? Was it possible she could love another besides the one she knew of, or was it something else? There was only one way to find out, she went and met with Jonee, and what she learned set her on a new path. Her memories became consistent, with visions and dreams, seeing a man in a kilt, who she believed was Connor, watching her regularly, and there were times she was sure she heard his voice when he spoke to her.

A Highlander's Love

One Saturday afternoon when Rebecca took a nap, she had a
dream —

*I am sitting on a bed with a woman standing in front of me,
and I have my hands on her legs moving them slowly up until I
reached the woman's perfect full breast, and when I reached her
face, I kissed her with such love and passion, a feeling I've never
felt before. It was so intense and powerful…I love her…no, not
her…this doesn't feel right. It feels wrong, so very wrong, and
then I realize I am not a man. I am a woman. Suddenly this
woman grabs my face and kisses me, and to my shock and
surprise, unlike what I felt before, this time, when I kissed her
back, it felt wrong. It felt so very wrong and disgusting. I quickly
pulled away, and when I did, the woman said, "you have never
kissed me like that before."*

Rebecca woke up stunned and shaken from what just
happened. She didn't understand why she had such a dream. It
felt strange and awkward as she thought, *this is wrong.* After a
few moments, she laid back down and went back to sleep, and to
her horror, she immediately returned to the dream.

*There is a man, the same man I've seen before, but he looked
distorted as if I am seeing him through a mirror, and it appeared
he is looking at himself in a mirror, but it was clear he couldn't
see me, as I expected him to. I decided to take advantage of the
fact that he could not see me, and took a good look at him. He is
a very handsome man, very handsome indeed. He is tall with
long brown wavy hair that was parted down the middle and fell
past his shoulders. He has a small mustache as I've seen in the
three-musketeer movie, and behind him, was a tall woman with
long dark wavy hair, that fell past her waist. I realize it was 'the
woman, and she was on her knees sitting on the bed.* Rebecca
woke up.

"What the hell was that?" Rebecca said with shock. "That
did not feel like a dream. It felt…I've felt this before with
Marco…as if I was actually there. In the first dream I appeared
to be a man, then the second time, I was watching with what

appeared…I was inside the mirror watching the man looking at himself."

This realization stunned Rebecca. When this happened before, it was within her time, but this time, it felt as if she – her soul traveled back in time, but this wasn't possible, *was it*? For a long time, Rebecca sat on the edge of her bed running through what happened. *Is it possible? Did I travel back in time…again? And to this same man, but in a different time. He appeared to be much older. I know my gift…my powers have become stronger, but…is this possible? Yes, yes of course it is, but why, and why now?*

Rebecca looked around her room as if she didn't recognize the place. When this happened – no, nothing like 'this' happened before, this was completely different. She wasn't just dreaming of the past, she was able to astral project her spirit to the past as well. Was this a sign of her power increasing or was it something else?

Rebecca did wonder if maybe this dream was her remembering a life when she lived as a man – *No! It didn't feel like that. It felt as if I actually traveled through time and space. I need to know if this is possible.*

It was possible, Rebecca did travel back in time, she was one of a few who were gifted with such a power. After all, time has no beginning or ending, everything is happening simultaneously, the past, the present, and the future. Time does not exist on the spiritual plain as it does for us on the earthly plain.

Chapter 16

Connor

Connor was sitting at the head of the table in the great room with his top men planning their next attack on the English who were trying to steal their lands.

"We need to form a plan to stop the English from taking Dunnottar Castle," Connor said.

"Aye, My Lord. Dunnottar is well fortified, with the only way in from the open sea. Do ye think they will come from the sea?" said Will, Connor's new captain.

"Aye, tis possible. We need to set guards below the castle at the sea edge and archers at the top of the castle walls and from each window," said Connor – William. He no longer allowed anyone, even his oldest friends and household to call him Connor. It was too much of a memory of the life he lost when he lost Heather.

"Aye, it will be done," said Will.

"Do we know where the English are now?" William asked.

"Aye, My Lord. The word came this morning that the English had entered Edinburgh."

"Then they could be here on the fourth night unless they go to Inverness first."

"Aye, which I believe they will," said Ian.

"Then we have time to prepare. Call the clans to Dunnottar Castle and prepare an attack they will never forget when the English arrive."

"Aye, it will be done My Lord," said Will.

Rebecca – October 2017

Rebecca was sitting on her sofa reading a book when she felt that all too familiar feeling in her heart, it was the same as she felt with Marco when their spirits connected. This one though, this one was different. It, in a way, reminded her of what she felt when one morning she saw a man at the place she goes for her hot Americano coffee, with a connection that pierced her heart with the word *family* whispering in her mind. At first, they didn't talk, but when they did, it confirmed what she was feeling – it was a family connection and she believed this man had a similar reaction, but it was never discussed, nor on any of the few times they saw each other after.

So, when Rebecca had that similar feeling with the thought of this man, she wondered, *is it possible, could it be him?* As soon as she had this thought, she shook her head, *no, that doesn't seem right. That man felt like family…a brother. This feeling, this feels like…love, in the way I felt with Marco.*

When the feeling wouldn't leave her, but instead grew stronger, feeling as if her spirit was being pulled from her body, without understanding why, nor did she have any control over it. She felt as if she was going to faint, and the ringing in her ears went from a soft hum – something she'd become accustomed to, when she learned the hum was her connection to the spiritual realm – to a loud ringing as if the universe was screaming at her. Rebecca placed her hand on her forehead and began to rub constantly as if she could smooth away whatever was happening to her.

However, Rebecca learned from her previous experience that when this happened it was best to go with it, instead of fighting it. So, Rebecca closed her eyes and when she did, she saw green mountains and felt they were of the Highland Mountains, ones she saw in a previous vision she believed were of a past life.

There, standing on the edge of a cliff was a woman with fire-red and orange hair. She appeared to be of noble blood, and Rebecca felt the woman lived at Dunnottar Castle, in what she believed was during the 1600s. The woman was standing in the grass at the edge of the cliff with a man, who she believed was Connor watching her – then the vision shifted, and she was watching Connor standing at the edge of the hill staring out to sea and calling – no, he was yelling Heather's name with desperation in his voice. Then suddenly, without any control,

Rebecca's spirit was whisked out of her body and found herself in spirit form, standing in the same place where the red-haired woman was standing. Shocked, then she had this need to call to the man she believed was Connor.

"Connor?" she yelled, but her voice wasn't her own, but one that was softer and more delegate, that she believed was the voice of the woman she use to be – his wife.

Connor was standing at the cliff looking out to the sea as he was thinking about Heather, which was something he's done every year since her death. She was his heart, his life, so when she died that day, so did he. Yes, he lived, but barely, and he missed her with every breath he took, to where he was living a half-life without her.

As Connor thought about how he lost Heather, anger stirred in him, and he was unable to hold back his anger any longer. He took a deep breath, then yelled at the top of his lungs, calling, nae, demanding she return to him. He did this with more power he ever thought or imagined was possible, and as he was filled with a tremendous amount of love and pain, his voice carried to the mountains and across the sea, even further, far into the universe, piercing through time and space, connecting to Rebecca's soul and heart, and when Connor heard his name from a voice that was familiar to him, he thought, *Heather.*

Connor whirled around so fast it almost caused him to lose his balance, and to his shock and surprise, he saw the woman he'd loved and grieved for standing before him, looking as she did when he last saw her, causing his heart to sink deep in his gut. With shock and wonder, *how is this possible?* Then, without further questions, he went to her and took her in his arms, and to his shock and surprise, *oh God, she is solid. She is real.*

When Connor grabbed Rebecca, she was shocked that he could touch her, and even more shocked she could feel him. She knew this was impossible since she was sure she was there in spirit, and in this form, no one should be able to touch her, let alone see her, so she wondered how this was possible. For

Rebecca to feel Connor's arms around her, as he held her tight against his body, she couldn't deny how good and right it felt.

In a shaky and shocking voice, she said, "Connor, I am sorry."

Connor was in disbelief, with tears running down his face, as his emotions were overwhelming him, at the same time, he was happy and overjoyed to have his Heather back and in his arms. He wanted to hold her and never let her go.

"Ye are here," he said filled with emotions, as tears were running down his face. "How can ye be here? How can I be touching ye? I am. I am touching ye. Do no leave me," he pleaded, tightening his hold on her. He believed if he held her tight enough, he wouldn't lose her again. "Do no leave me. Stay with me," he begged with pain and anguish in his voice, at the same time filled with joy.

When Rebecca heard Connor's pain, the last thing she wanted to do was cause this man who had already suffered, any further pain than she already had by her being there, and the pain it will cause when she leaves, because she knew she couldn't stay.

"I cannot Connor. I am not sure why or how I am here, but I am no longer a part of this world…your world. From where I'm from, I was able to feel your pain. It called to me, and now here I am standing in your arms. I do not know how this is possible."

Rebecca had feelings for this man she didn't understand. For a man she didn't know, nor did he hold the soul of Marco. Without understanding why, she felt a strong and powerful connection to this man, and being with him in his arms, here in the past, she knew she was the one who hurt him, and she wanted to find a way to help him heal. He needed to let her go, and he needed to live, not only for her but for himself as well. She doesn't only want him to live, but she needed him to love again as well, by opening his heart to allow another into his life.

Rebecca suddenly felt her spirit wavering, with the need to return to her body, but she had to tell him before it was too late.

"Please Connor, live. Live for me. Love again. Don't allow what I did…my death to end yours."

Filled with fear, *NO! She can no leave me,* he thought. Connor could not lose her again. "No!" he yelled, as he desperately tried to hold Heather tight against him, refusing to let her go. "Ye can no leave me! I need ye! There will be no other!"

Rebecca – Heather could feel his fear, pain, and anguish at the thought of losing her – again, but she knew she couldn't stay. This was no longer her time nor her world, and this, she must make him understand.

"I cannot stay. I am of another world, another lifetime. I cannot stay!" she said again and loud enough so he would hear her.

Panicked, "NO!" Connor yelled again as he increased his hold on her, hoping in doing so, he could hold her to him, thus preventing her from leaving him – again.

Rebecca's heart broke for Connor, she knew she could not stay, but at the same time, she wanted to stay and be what he needed. How could she, she has another life, in another time. She was no longer a part of his time.

"Connor, I love you and I always will, but I must return before it's too late. I am sorry Connor," she said with pain and sorrow in her voice. She loved this man with all her heart. It was strange though since she believed Marco was her heart and soul, there could never be, nor have there ever been another. But here, with this man, how could she deny it – it was possible. "Live. Live for me. Love again. Open your heart. Please Connor, for me," Rebecca pleaded, feeling her time was coming to an end, with her spirit needing to return.

Connor refused to let her go, as he could feel her spirit slipping away from his hold – slipping through his arms. "No!" he yelled, but it was too late, Rebecca's spirit was gone.

When Rebecca returned to her body in the twenty-first century, she was left feeling weak, more so than at other times when she left her body. She was afraid that if she didn't return when she did, her body would have been an empty shell, lost to her world forever, but it also left her heart aching for Connor, and a little guilty for leaving him with the pain and anguish he was feeling.

This is all my fault. I must make right the wrong I did. How could I have known…allowed my sorrow to control me. I had no idea of the pain I was leaving behind when, as Heather, I took my own life.

Chapter 17

When Heather – Rebecca disappeared, Connor was left bereft, with his heart caught in his throat, then heartbroken turned to anger. This was his chance to tell Heather how he felt about her and how lost he's been without her. This was his moment and now she was gone. "Why?" he said aloud.

"Because she was no of this time. Yer grieving drew her soul to ye, but she lives in another time. In another place. She can no be with ye now," said the Fae.

When Connor heard the voice of the old woman, he spun around and saw her standing there at the edge of the forest and wondered, *what is she doing here? How did she get here?* Connor looked around trying to see where she came from when only moments ago he was alone with Heather.

"What do ye know of this old woman!" he said in a firm and demanding voice. "Who are ye!"

Connor's anger and demands did not affect the old woman, after all, Connor was given a gift, a great gift, and the Fae smiled, "Connor, do ye truly want to know who I am? If so, I shall tell ye," she said, watching him with raised eyebrows.

Of course he wanted to know who this woman was, after all, she seemed to appear right out of thin air. "Yes! Tell me now!" he demanded.

She smiled and said, "I am Fae," and stopped to allow that one word to sink in.

Connor stood there staring at the old woman with shock on his face, unsure what to think or believe. What was he to say. "Fae?" he said slowly and softly, as if she might be mad and required a quiet and easy voice. *She's mad,* he thought. Then he tried to say, "they do no," but then stopped, what was he going to say, *they do no exist,* but then how could he explain what happened and how she could suddenly be there as if she appeared from thin air? In all these years of seeing this old woman, each time felt like the first.

The old woman – Fae smiled, "ah, but we do."

Connor lowered his head, then in a whisper, "ye are the one who brought Heather back to me. Why? Why do so, then take her away from me?"

"Connor, it was no I who brought her to ye. It was ye. Yer pain. Yer heartbreak called to her spirit. Ye called her to ye. Ye brought Heather here. I told ye once before, ye would see her again, but she would be different. Do ye remember?" she asked, then in a soft whisper, not intended for Connor to hear, "but this was no the look I expected," she said, expecting Heather to appear as her future self, going by the name of Rebecca.

Connor raised his head, shocked at what the Fae said, *how tis possible?* he thought. Connor remembered the night this old woman – Fae told him he would see Heather again, of course, he didn't believe her, but now, could he?

"How?" he asked. "I do no have the power to do such a thing." Then he remembered what he heard the Fae whisper, "wait, ye said…I heard ye say she did no look as ye expected her to look. What do ye mean?"

The Fae smiled and said, "aye, but ye do, yer heart and soul connected to hers. Yer love called to her heart and her soul. No matter where her soul is, it connected and brought her to ye. Tis is a very strong power…love. Tis odd though, as ye are no the one her soul is bound to," she said. "The woman I expected ye to see was the woman Heather's soul is now, in the time she lives now, no as she looked when she lived as Heather. Tis, I can only understand, tis what yer heart wanted…needed to see, so it did," the Fae explained.

To hear this overwhelmed Connor, shocked at what he heard. He shook his head as he thought, *this makes no sense,* then he said aloud, "me? How," shaking his head again, "can I do it again? Bring her back to me…to life again. Here in this time?" he said with hope in his heart. Connor then thought, *no, this is mad,* and then he remembered what the Fae said, "how can ye say I am no the one bound to her soul?" he asked, with confusion.

"Tis, I am afraid I can no answer either. What I can tell ye, Heather, who is Rebecca in this other life, will be traveling from what ye call the Americas, the new land, to Scotland and will visit Dunnottar Castle. Tis possible, when this happens there will be another connection between ye both," she said, then right before Connor's eyes, with a smile, she vanished into thin air.

Connor spun around looking everywhere to where the old woman went to, but he could not deny that she disappeared using magic – Fae magic. *Tis true. In all these years I could no really believe…but tis true, she is Fae.* Although he's had other encounters and has seen her disappear before, this time, this time, he finally saw the truth and believed in what he saw.

After Connor returned to the castle, he ignored everyone, including his wife Sophia who called out to him, going directly to his bedchamber, not in the mood to deal with her or anyone else at that moment.

Recently, Sophia told him he was going to be a father, and he wanted to be happy, but instead, he felt sad and disappointed. It was supposed to be Heather having his child, his heir, not this woman he doesn't even love. Unfortunately, after three years of marriage to Heather, it was not to be. He never understood why, nor did she. Yes, he wanted a child, and if God didn't bless them with a child, he would have been satisfied with only Heather. Now, to have to deal with Sophia being with child, instead of feeling joy, he was filled with pain, sorrow, and disappointment. Yes, Sophia may give him an heir, which was good for his clan, but it wasn't Heather caring for his child, and that mattered more to him than he realized, which made the loss of Heather that much more painful than it had been before.

And after seeing her and touching her…it should be her…Heather, he thought.

Did it bother him? Yes, of course, it did, and he did everything he could to avoid his wife. Did he feel shame for this? Yes and no. The simple thing was, he just didn't care. If he had an heir, then he did his duty as laird, and then, just maybe, he could join Heather, but then he heard a voice, her voice, *no Connor, you cannot take your life. You must live.*

Filled with great sorrow, Connor opened the door to his bedchamber, and after shutting it, he went and collapsed on his chair near the window that overlooked the sea. He looked out to the night sky and the stars shining above, seeking the heavens, wondering how it was possible with what happened on the cliff, and how he had this power the Fae mentioned, and could he do it again.

"What am I to do? How can I live and love, when the one I gave my heart to is gone? Who is now living in another time? Can I…is it possible…can I call her back?" he said to the night air, shaking his head, "should I? Is it right? Is it fair to her? To me?"

As Connor sat contemplating these questions, he fell asleep and slipped into a dream world where he found Heather – Rebecca.

Connor found himself in a far-off land, one he had never seen before. There were things – objects he was unfamiliar with. There were metal contraptions that could travel a great distance, faster than the fastest horse he has ridden, and then, there she was, the woman he's never seen before, yet familiar to him. As he watches this woman, he sees flashes of Heather, his Heather, as if her spirit was overlapping this woman before him. She has long dark curly – no, not curly, but wavy hair. She has beautiful brown eyes, and her lips, ones he's inclined to kiss… "Wait! Who is she? Can it be? Tis possible, this woman is Heather?"

Rebecca was in her car driving home from work when she felt as if someone was with her. *Marco?* she thought since when she's had these feelings in the past, was when she felt Marco's spirit with her, but there was something different, something she didn't recognize. It was another. *Who?* she wondered, but then, *no, it must be Marco.*

As Connor watched Rebecca, without realizing what he was doing, he reached his hand out with the need to touch her, and before he knew it, he softly caressed the side of her face and was surprised he was able to feel her, and then, unable to stop himself, he tried to kiss her neck, in a place he knew his Heather liked. Then to his wonder, Rebecca put her hand over the place he kissed. *She felt my kiss,* he thought with shock. To be sure it wasn't his imagination, Connor kissed her again, but this time he lingered, relishing in the feel of her, and when he saw Rebecca smile, he knew she liked what he was doing, but then he heard, "Marco, I know it's you. You are here?" To hear this, shocked Connor awake.

When Connor woke, he felt confused, and when he looked at where he was, he was surprised to see he was still in his chair. He rubbed his face as he tried to understand what happened. "Lord, what was that? It was her…Heather. How? Was this what the Fae said, tis Heather, but different.

Chapter 18

Rebecca – Fall 2017

Since her first dream of this man in the highlands, Rebecca has been dreaming or having visions of a life she lived in the highlands during the early to mid-1600s. Although she went through it in 2013, this time though, this was different. She wasn't only remembering and feeling a life from before, her spirit was able to travel to the past, to the man she believed was her husband when she lived in the highlands, and her feelings for the man were even more powerful than what she felt for Marco.

How can this be? she thought.

"I felt him, I know I did. But how and why? Who is he and where is he?" Rebecca said to the ceiling above her bed. "I will meet with Jonee again. I am sure she will have the answers this time. I must believe it."

The following morning Rebecca texted Jonee and scheduled an appointment that afternoon and when she arrived, they went through their normal introductions.

"Hi Rebecca, how are you?" Jonee asked.

"I'm doing well, thank you."

"Well, you know where to go, and when you are ready, we will get started."

"Okay."

Jonee began her prayer and when she was ready, she went through the usual reading of Rebecca's aura, the things that were going on in her life, and after, Rebecca asked her question.

"In this past life of the highlands, I'm not only remembering and feeling, but my spirit is also traveling to that time. Is that even possible?"

"Yes, of course, it is. There is no time, as the time in the past is happening, so is the present, as is the future."

"Yes, this I am aware of. I feel that I need to make right the wrong I did in that former life. To help my…her husband to heal and forgive. I feel I will meet him, that he's been reborn in this time… in life."

"Yes and no. It is strange. It's as if he is not born…yet…he is. This tells me, although he is born, his soul is between two worlds. The spiritual and the physical."

Rebecca was stunned to hear this and asked, "is that possible."

"Yes. If they choose to be part of both worlds, it is possible. This tells me his gift is strong since it allows his soul to be a part of both worlds."

This is maddening. How can this be possible? So much is happening I don't understand, she thought but chose to say nothing.

"He chose this. It was a way for him to help you. In helping you, it would be helping himself. This is to allow him to find you. He is helping you remember your lives together during that time."

Wow! My heart jumps at the idea of what he is doing. There must be something I can do. "Is there anything I should be doing?" Rebecca asked.

"No. Just keep doing what you are doing, and in time all will be revealed." There was a small pause, then she said, "you must go to Scotland. There is something there you must find. This will help you…there is nothing else…only…I am getting…you must go to Scotland, and when you do, plan for it to be extended."

Chills just ran through my body at the word Scotland, along with excitement at the possibilities of what might happen when I am there. "Okay. It's funny you should say that, as I have been getting that exact same feeling."

"Well, is there anything else?"

Anything else? There are tons of questions I want to ask, but there just isn't enough time, she thought, but said, "No, thank you."

"Okay, I am going to close and then you can pay me."

"Okay, thank you."

Jonee closed the connection to the spiritual world, and after Rebecca paid her, she left. While she was driving home, her mind was swarming with the possibilities of what was going to happen when she goes to Scotland. Then, much later, Rebecca remembered how she felt about a man who works in her office building – a connection she felt deep in her heart, and she knew he felt it as well, when he looked at her with shock and recognition, but he didn't stop, nor did she try to stop him.

It was much later that she realized Connor was using men close to her to be able to see her with human eyes.

There were times when Rebecca felt sad or lonely, and when this happened, he was there. All she had to do was close her eyes and think of him, and he was there. He, who she believed to be Connor when his name came to her that day and eventually became her highlander.

During these times of sadness, Connor would place his arms around Rebecca, and for Rebecca, it truly felt as if he was holding her close to his chest, with the need to comfort her. It felt as if he was really there with her. She knew it wasn't possible, yet it was. *Haven't you learned; anything is possible?* It's not like this was her first experience, it's happened before with Marco, yet, this time, this time it was different. Somehow, five hundred years in the past he was able to stretch through time and space when he felt her need for him. Did Rebecca call to him? Maybe it wasn't her, but her soul. But it wasn't just Connor, it was Rebecca as well, when she felt his need for her, she would – in spirit, go to him.

The problem with this, it wasn't her calling Connor from the past, it was his spirit that was coming to her. An experience that was unheard of. Something that we as humans believed to be impossible. So why now? Why her? Why both of them? Many questions she had no answers to.

One day while Rebecca was at work, she had a vision and saw Connor standing on the cliff —

Connor

Connor was standing on the cliff that was once his and Heather's favorite place when she was alive, and now, it was no longer his favorite place, but the place that claimed the life of his wife, which was now known to him as Heather's Cliff. A place he could go when he needed to be close to Heather or speak to her.

"Heather, my love, I am still amazed at the wonderful miracle, nae, gift ye have given me. In the years since yer death, when I lost ye, tis been very difficult," he said lowering his head in shame with sorrow in his heart, of the decision he made all those years ago that led to her death. "Here, in this place, I can feel ye and know ye are with me," he said with a tear rolling down his face. "My heart aches for ye, and tis always will. I have done what ye asked of me, I have tried to open my heart to another…my wife. The woman I married…well, was forced to marry by the king of France. It was an offering of his goodwill," he said with a sigh. "Heather, my love, know I will never forget ye. Never. Ye are my heart and soul, and when my time comes, I shall find ye. I know this to be true. Wait for me love. Wait, knowing I shall join ye wherever ye may be. I am trying to do what ye asked of me to love again, but my love, I am finding it difficult, but I am trying."

Connor heard a noise, and when he turned around, he was hoping to see Heather, but instead, it was his wife, Sophia.

"Husband, what are you doing here?" she asked looking around at the small cliff.

"Wife, what are ye doing here? Ye should no be here," he said with anger. *How dare she come to this place that belongs to me and Heather. No her,* he thought, as his anger grew.

This is a sacred place; one no one should visit except him.

"Husband, why does my appearance anger you so?" Sophia asked with concern in her voice.

Connor took a few moments to gather his anger, forcing it down where it belongs. "Forgive me wife, but ye should no be here. Tis a sacred place and ye no belong here."

Sophia was told of this place by the housekeeper and about what happened after she forced the housekeeper by threatening to get rid of her if she didn't. Up until now, she has respected his wishes, but after the change in his behavior and with the birth of their child coming, she needed to confront him about this.

After time, Sophia fell in love with Connor. No, he wasn't always kind, but he had a good heart and when she saw the way he treated his people, she couldn't help but love him, and she wished, in time, he would return the love.

"William, I do not wish to anger you…I know why you come here. Will you not share your grief with me, your wife?" she asked.

Connor was shocked, he had no idea she knew why he came to this place, but at the same time, he was not surprised. *She must have hounded the staff until they gave in and told her the story.*

"This here," pointing at the ground, "is my business, no yers. I no wish to speak of it, and ye will no return to this place again," he said with a snap.

"William, I am your wife, will you not share your grief with me? Allow me to help you heal the pain in your heart? We are soon," placing her hand over her round belly, "we will have a child, a son, who will, if I am unable to, fill your heart with love." Sophia walked over and placed her other hand on his arm, "and one day, you will open your heart to me, and allow me to love you as I already do."

Connor did not know what to say. How can this woman love him when all he's shown her was a man with a void of feelings – a cold heart? This woman from the future, told him to love again, but can he? Is it possible? Shaking his head, *nae, tis no possible. I can no love this woman when Heather holds my heart.*

Connor took Sophia's hand and placed it in the crook of his, "come, let us return to the castle." Without a word, they walked away from the cliff and returned to the castle.

Connor was standing alone in the great hall of Dunnottar Castle wearing his war regalia after meeting with his men, as he contemplated on the battle that lay ahead. It was 1655, and once again they were getting ready to defend Scotland against the English, *tis to be the battle I will fall in?"* he wondered. More than once, Connor thought about taking his life and joining his beloved Heather, until he remembered how she somehow, and in some way, she'd been there for him and loved him from afar. Although he never understood it, he knew it to be true, and so it was decided, on this big battle he would fall and die as the highland warrior he was. And with this, he suddenly felt her – Heather. Connor shook his head, *no, tis can no be. Aye, tis so, but no Heather, tis her.*

Yes, it was Rebecca, but not her physically, it was only her voice, her words in his mind.

Connor, you cannot die. I will not allow it. If you die, we cannot be together. You must live. Live for me...for us. It's not your time. You must fight as you did before, so you can return to me. Although I am not there now, I am here waiting for you. Live for us. I love you. I've never stopped. For you to be with me, and for us to be together, you must fight as the warrior you are. Fight for me. Fight for us, and return alive, and allow time to pass as it should, then, and only then, can we be together. Please Connor, for me? I love you, and I want you here with me. In this time. In this place. Fight, knowing you will return to me, but not in death, alive and in my time, she said, and then she was gone.

For Connor to hear Heather's – Rebecca's plea, how could he not survive. Resigned, he left the great hall to join his men as the powerful leader and the fierce highlander warrior he was.

"Men, let us go. By morning, we will engage in battle against the English.

The men roared in agreement and were eager to see battle so they could destroy those English fools.

Later that evening, "My Laird! My Laird! Ye must come at once!" yelled Mary the housemaid.

"What is it Mary, for ye to holler as if to wake the dead?" Connor asked.

"Yer wife, My Laird, tis time for her to give birth."

Connor's mouth dropped open, what was he to do? "Why do ye come to me Mary, is no the midwife with Sophia."

"Aye, but she is calling for ye, My Laird."

"She no need me," he said, then turned and left the castle and headed to the cliff.

Mary was left stunned by what he said and did, but now was not the time to concern herself with her laird's decision, so she turned and went quickly to be by Sophia's side.

When Mary entered the room —

"Where is William?" Sophia called.

Mary, unable to look at her, lowered her head and said, "My Lady, I could no find him. He must be out preparing to leave for battle on the morrow."

Sophia, for a long moment just stared at Mary, knowing what the truth was, and he refused to come. "Very well Mary, come and hold my hand."

Mary curtsied and quickly made her way to her lady's bedside.

Connor was standing on the cliff looking out to sea, "I can no do this. I can no watch another woman have my child when it should be ye having my child. No I can no do it."

"Lad, ye can and ye will," said the Fae.

"Why am I no surprised to hear ye old woman," Connor said.

"Aye, ye no surprised at my presence anymore."

"Nae, no more."

"Ah, tis good then."

"Why are ye here old woman?" he asked.

Turning in the direction of the castle, "ye need to go to yer wife Connor. She needs ye. She is giving birth to yer son and heir."

Surprised, "then it is a son," he said. "A son," shaking his head, "nae, tis should have been Heather that gave me a son, no Sophia."

"Nae Connor, she could no have given ye a son, she was barren."

Connor snapped his head to look at the old woman, "nae, tis no so," he said, but he knew it was true, after all, in the three years they were married she did not get pregnant when most women did after the first few months of being married if not sooner.

"Aye, ye no tis true. In that castle is yer wife who is giving ye yer heir, and instead of being there by her side as she needs ye to be, ye are here thinking of a past long gone."

This made Connor angry, "watch yer mouth, old woman. Fae or no Fae, I will cut ye down."

The Fae laughed, "aye, ye would strike down a defenseless old woman? Aye, ye will no do so. I am Fae and ye can no harm me."

Lowering his head in shame, "aye, tis so. I could no harm ye. Fae or no Fae. I can no go to Sophia. I can no watch her give birth to my son."

"Aye, ye can and ye will."

Connor, for a long moment just stared in the direction of the castle as he thought, *can I? Can I go and watch Sophia give birth to my son? Nae, I can no do it.* But then, Connor turned to the Fae, he knew she was right, and so he finally gave in, "aye, ye are right," he said looking back at the castle.

"What are ye waiting for? Go, ye fool."

Connor smiled and started towards the castle and to Sophia's bedside.

When Connor returned to the castle and entered Sophia's bedchamber, he heard his son let out a loud cry, and when the midwife turned around, "My Laird, ye have yerself a son and heir," she said with excitement.

Connor couldn't help it, he smiled and quickly went to his son, and after the midwife cleaned and wrapped him in a blanket, she placed him in Connor's arms. "My son," he said with amazement.

"Aye, he is your son. Best late than never," Sophia said.

For the first time, Connor looked at Sophia, "aye," he said moving to her bedside and sat on the edge of the bed. "He is healthy."

"He is, and he needs to be fed. Hand him to me," she said, stretching out her arms.

Connor looked at Sophia, reluctant to let his son go, but he did as she bid. Once he handed his son to his wife, he watched her place his son to her breast and was amazed at how quickly his son latched on to her nipple and began sucking fiercely, causing Connor to laugh. "Aye, tis my son, he is."

"That he is. What shall we name him," Sophia asked?

"We shall name him Gordon William Keith. Gordon after my friend and William for my father."

Sophia smiled, "that is a wonderful name. From this day, our son will be known as Gordon William Keith."

Everyone in the room cheered and word spread through the castle announcing that the first son and heir has been born. It was a wonderful celebration of life before he and his men went off to battle.

"Tis, I believe another reason for him to live," said the Fae.

Standing at the edge of the battlefield Connor's mind went back to what he heard – to what she said. *Tis no easy. Why can I no fall in battle, did I no live long enough? Do I no deserve to rest and be with my beloved Heather once again? I gave my clan an heir, and when he is of age he will take over as laird. There are those who will see to his education and training,* he thought, but in the middle of his thoughts, he heard a familiar voice in his mind. *Ye a fool, ye know! Ye must live, die when he deems time, no ye!* It was the old woman – the Fae.

Connor looked around, expecting to see the old woman, but she was nowhere to be found, but then he heard her laughter, *ye fool, I am no there, but in yer mind, as ye well know. I am Fae.* Then she was gone, so he thought.

Connor shook his head, "I am going mad," he said under his breath, so no other could hear him. *No, ye are no going mad!"* said the old woman in his mind, then she was truly gone. *Very well. I shall fight as the warrior I am and live for her. The one from the future.*

And he did. He fought like the fierce warrior he was, and although defeated once again by the English, he went home with his head held high, knowing he survived. He didn't do it for himself, but for her – Heather. *No no Heather, tis Rebecca.*

Chapter 19

<u>Rebecca</u>

Rebecca was resting in her bed watching a movie when she had that all too familiar feeling, one she has now come to recognize as him – Connor. She gathered herself for what she knew was to come, so she laid back on her bed and closed her eyes, allowing her soul to take her to where she needed to be, and when she arrived, she could feel Connor's sadness.

<u>Christmas in the Highlands</u>

When it came to Christmas, although Connor participated in the festivities, his heart and soul were never fully there. Yes, he made sure to make merriment with his wife, son, and clan, but hidden deep, he could never forget the years he spent with Heather, his true wife. Yes, he opened his heart to love again, but he could never fully give Sophia his heart since a part of his heart would always belong to Heather.

Sophia knew when Connor decided to give her his heart, it was also the time he explained everything to her, about his first wife, and how Heather would always be a part of his heart. Although he was giving her his heart, she wouldn't own it completely, and to Connor's surprise, Sophia understood and didn't ask for anything more than what he was willing to give. Sophia proved to be a good, devoted, and honorable wife and mother, more than he could have ever asked for.

During the festivities, Connor was standing near a window that was far away from the others, looking out to the snow-covered night as he thought of Heather – missing her when to his shock, he heard 'her' voice.

Connor my love, I am here with you and can feel your sorrow. Know this, my love, I understand, and I am always here for you. You will always own a part of my heart. Merry Christmas my love. I love you and I always will.

Connor released his breath he didn't realize he was holding when he heard Rebecca's voice, and it always amazed him how she always seemed to know when he needed her as if his soul called to hers. *I will never forget ye love. When this holy day comes, how can I no think of ye. Happy Christmas love. Ye are my heart and soul. One day we shall be together again. I love ye Rebec-ca,* he said, stuttering her name, when suddenly he felt a hand brush the side of his face. The feeling shocked him, as he heard, *never forget. Live and love. I will be here waiting for you,* then he felt her hand on his chest, resting directly over his heart and she said, *I will always be here, a part of your heart, as you will always be a part of mine.* When Connor heard this, he could feel her head resting against his chest, directly over his heart, and when this happened, he was surprised to find tears running down his face. *Never forget, as I will never forget, I love you, Connor, always and forever,* she said, and then she was gone.

When Connor returned to the present, he found he was looking in the direction of his clan enjoying the holiday festivities and when he saw his wife, he quickly turned away, not wanting their – her eyes on him, so he turned back towards the window and looked out and allowed the tears to fall once again. No, it wasn't all from sadness, from happiness as well. "Thank you for such a gift," he whispered.

After taking a few more moments to gather himself, he once again turned to face his clan and family, and when he did, he noticed his wife was watching him, and without delay, he went to join her and his son. When he arrived, Connor took her outstretched hand and said, "I am alright love."

"I have no doubt, my love. Sit, and take in the merriment."

Connor did, as he gathered his son on his lap.

<u>Rebecca</u>

When Rebecca returned to the present, she was left feeling happy, yet sad as well. She didn't know Connor, but, in some way, she loved him, and she wondered how she would feel when she made her trip to Scotland to see Dunnottar Castle.

Just after the New Year, Connor was on the cliff staring out to the sea when he heard a voice from behind him.

"Ye share a soul. Ye and this other man, tis what ties ye to Heather – Rebecca," the Fae explained to Connor.

"How tis that possible? How can a soul be two people? Two men? Two men, my Heather…this Rebecca is connected to? How is she to choose?" he asked. What he was hearing, was beyond his comprehension and understanding.

"There is no real way to explain this to ye. I have no seen it, I have heard tis was possible. She is tied to ye both because ye are both of the same soul, "the Fae said.

"Can she love us both? How can she choose?" he said, and then asked as he shook his head in disbelief, "what does it matter, she is of another time. A time, I can no be a part of. She lives and she lives with…him," he said with a lump in his throat, as his heart was breaking, and what he heard next shocked him.

"She is no with this other man," she said with a smile on her face.

"What? When I was with her in my dream, she called his name."

"Aye, but he has no found his way to her yet, and there is a chance he never will."

With hope, Connor said, "then tis possible…we can find each other again, in this other life?"

The Fae smiled and said, "aye, but it will no be easy. When ye arrive in that time ye will no remember. It will be ye who will need to recognize her. Yer heart will tell ye. It will recognize her, but will ye fear it or will ye embrace it? This man…this other man was once open to this love, but he struggled because he no understood what was happening and allowed his mind to rule him instead of listening to his heart. If he had, he would have been with her already, now, in her time, the time ye saw her in. It will be up to ye and how strong yer heart is. Will ye listen to yer heart versus yer mind," she said.

"How will," he began to say but wiped away that thought from his mind. "I will, when I meet God, I will ask him to help me know the truth."

"Ye may no have a choice," she said, then, "but, if I help ye, tis possible."

Connor looked at the old woman, not understanding what she could mean. "What say ye, old woman?"

The Fae smiled, "aye, tis no for me to say. I have much to think…to consider. Ye will know on the day of yer death," she said, then turned and walked towards the forest.

"Wait! Ye must tell me."

But the old woman ignored him and only raised her hand before disappearing behind the forest trees.

The power of Fae magic is one no one – no human could ever understand. The Fae was a powerful one of her kind, and although it's been many centuries since she lived freely among her people, and when most power would diminish with time living in the human world, it wasn't so for this old woman – Fae. Instead, she has managed to maintain her power and the power to do what she says. Connor will share a soul with this other man, but not in the way one would believe, but a part – a piece of this other man, who is of his time, known as William Booth, is a part of Connor, thus why this other man could never fully commit to Rebecca, because that part that is of Connor, prevents him from doing so, in a way no living being could ever comprehend.

For the next several years Connor honored Heather, by doing what she asked of him – he lived. He lived for her, and he lived for himself, but most of all, he lived. Connor's son, who chose to use the name William, grew to be a great man, and when he was gone, he would be a great laird, as his time grew close, now that he was an old man and his time was close at hand, and soon he will be with his Heather once again.

Chapter 20

Rebecca – Dunnottar Castle, Scotland 2018

"Finally, I can't believe I am finally here in Scotland and at Dunnottar Castle, the place I've been dreaming about," Rebecca said as she sat in her rented car looking at the castle in the distance.

Rebecca arrived at Dunnottar Castle as the sun began to rise because she wanted to walk the ruined castle alone before others arrived, and when she first saw the magnificent Castle, it felt like home, as she felt when she first saw Dunham Massey Castle in Cheshire, England when she visited in 2013 right before her memories of her first past life began to haunt her everyday life.

When Rebecca finally gathered her courage to leave her car, she began to walk the path that led to the castle, when her attention was pulled to her right, a path that led in the direction of a cliff. She hesitated for a few moments, she knew what that cliff was, so after she gathered the courage, she began to walk the path, and as she did so, fear began to creep up inside of her, and the closer she came to the cliff, she had to stop, finding she couldn't go any further.

"This is it, the place I…Heather took her life."

Rebecca tried to move closer to the cliff but found she could go no more than a few feet before the cliff edge. So, instead, she just stood there staring at the place for a long time, before her attention drew her to the right, where she was sure there used to be a grand forest, but was now open land with homes spread out in the distance. After a time, Rebecca could no longer remain on the cliff, and when she looked in the direction of the castle, she knew it was time.

When Rebecca reached the steps that led to the base of the castle, she could not believe the number of steps there were, and once she made it down to the first landing, she had to take a breath, and once she was down the rest of the stairs, she slowly made her way up the long walkway to the first set of uneven cobblestone that would lead to the castle entrance. After taking the first few steps to the first landing, she looked to a room that was on her right, and when she looked inside, although she felt the need to go in, she decided against it and continued on the path that took her up several more steps to the tower gatehouse, where she purchased her ticket to enter the castle grounds, and had her first feeling of a time past.

As Rebecca entered the courtyard she felt 'him', he was there with her, and then she heard his voice, *aye love, I am here with ye.* To her shock, he was talking in what she believed was his natural voice and accent, not at all what she heard before. Connor was walking by her side acting as her personal tour guide, telling about the places, pointing out buildings that looked to have once been small rooms, and Connor told her they were lodging for his men – his warriors, and when Rebecca looked at the sign of the description of what the building was, to her shocked, it was what he said. If she had any doubts before, this cleared that up, Connor was by her side, telling her about the place, and making her laugh at some of the antics he and his men use to play when they were young.

As Rebecca walked the grounds and roamed the castle ruins, her mind was flooded with memories of the life she lived when she was Heather, and when she came to the countess suite and was about to enter, Connor tried to stop her, by convincing her it wasn't worth looking at and tried to push her to the chamber that use to be his, but she refused.

Ye can no go in there. Please love, do no go in there.

She had to go inside; she was sure this was the room she saw in her vision/dream. *I need to go inside. I must see and know the truth.* And she did. She ignored Connor's concerns and walked into the chamber, and when she did, the visions and dreams she had of this place came flooding back to her and when she looked beyond where the bed used to be to a small chamber in the back, she knew her memories were correct. That back room was the countess's dressing room and where her lady's maid slept when it was required of her to do so.

You were here with her…your wife when I saw you through the mirror.

Connor sighed, *aye, tis was. I did no want you to remember that. I feel shame ye had to see her with me.*

You have nothing to feel shame about. She was your wife and I…Heather was dead.

Will ye now come to my chamber?

Rebecca turned to the door and smiled, *yes,* and went into the room that used to be Connor's bedchambers, and right away she was drawn to the window, but before she went to the window, she looked at the room, and she was able to see how the room would have been set up. In her visions and dreams, she saw the bed was on the right of the room and the chair sat directly under the window, where she saw Connor sitting staring out when he thought of Heather. After a short time, Rebecca walked to the window and when she looked out, she saw what he saw – the sea, but not only the sea, the hope he felt knowing she was out there, across the sea and universe to another time and place, and she wanted to weep at the sadness he felt knowing he couldn't be with her, or her with him.

Nae love, do no weep. Tis how it was supposed to be. Nothing can change that.

I am sorry Connor. I am sorry I left you.

Nae love, ye have no reason to be sorry. One day we will be together again.

When Rebecca turned around, she saw a woman standing in the doorway waiting to take a picture, "oh, I am sorry. Let me get out of your way." Rebecca moved and when she looked at the fireplace and saw Connor's initials and the countesses, she wanted to cry, as she felt those initials should have been Heather's.

I am sorry love. Tis should have been yers and mine.

No, it is what it was meant to be. Without further communication, Rebecca continued to walk the castle and when she went into the brewery she smiled as scenes of laughter flooded her mind, with Connor whispering in her ear, *aye, we had a grand time here on many nights drinking and laughing.* And as Rebecca was looking around and hearing the fun they were having, she turned to see a man come in from the doorway off the small balcony.

"It's sad isn't it, to see a great castle in ruins."

"Yes, it is. I feel I know this place…it, well, it feels…"

"It was a wonderful place."

"Yes, and I am thinking of writing a story about this place, about the loss of a wife so young to a young highlander, who was lost to the world."

For a long moment, the man only stared at Rebecca, as if she had spoken words that she should not have known about, and decided to test her. "Yes, the wife and laird were a great couple during their time."

"No, not that wife, the first wife, the one…" Rebecca stopped herself, before revealing too much.

The man was surprised and only said, "oh, I see."

Rebecca saw the confusion and said, "I am creating a nonfiction story, a creation of my own. As I am walking the grounds, I am trying to think of how it would feel for the person who was reincarnated would feel to return to a place she lived a life before."

"Oh, yes, I see. Well, enjoy your visit," the man said, as he turned and left, going through the door he came in from.

Rebecca, not thinking twice, turned and headed out of the brewery to the room on the other side that had a large hole in the outer wall on the westside, and then, she turned back to where she came from, feeling that the man was something more than just a man, and the word that came in her mind was *Fae*. Rebecca shook her head and continued to the wall with the hole in it and when she touched the side of the opening, she felt a strange energy coming from the stones, and then there was an old woman standing right next to her.

The old woman was short, maybe four feet three inches, with short curly salt and pepper hair, and the old woman said, "You feel it don't you?"

"What do you mean?" Rebecca asked.

"You know what I mean. You feel the energy, don't you?"

"I feel something, yes. An energy…possibly."

"Nae, child, you feel the energy. You know what I mean."

Rebecca let out her breath, "I suppose I do, but what does it mean?"

"You understand," pointing at the hole, "this is a portal," she said. "A portal that will take you back to the time before he meets her. You can meet him and spend time…would that be something you'd be interested in?'

"What do you mean him?" *This old woman could not possibly know, could she?* Rebecca thought.

"Aye, you do."

"I don't know if it's possible. Even if it is, this," pointing at the hole," is a wall and on the other side is the sea. If I were to walk through or go through this…what you say is a portal, I would land in the sea."

"Ah yes, you are right about that, but child, you will live. You will live because you are protected. Nothing will happen to you. You will survive and you will be rescued by him."

"But why…why should I do this?"

"Because it is the right thing to do. It is something you must do."

"And if I do this what will happen?"

"You will know each other, and you will fall in love. He will know you as the woman of this time but love you as the woman of his."

"What could you mean?" Rebecca asked, confused by what this woman was saying, not understanding how this was possible.

"When you are together in his time, and then when you leave, the time you've spent together will be forgotten by both of you, so when he meets her, the one he is meant to be with, he will love her and she, not understanding why, will love him as well. She is you and you are her, although you are in different times, she the past and you the future, you are still one soul. She will feel what you felt, allowing them to be together."

"Is this even possible?"

"Yes, it is possible."

"But why would I do this, when it could only hurt myself?"

"No, because you are the beginning to their beginning of their time, to what will happen to you in your time. This must be done. Time must come together. The future to the past, the past to the future, tying both as one."

Rebecca felt so confused, but for some reason, she trusted this woman. As she stood in the center of the ruined room, she took a deep breath and closed her eyes to allow whatever brought her to Dunnottar Castle to guide her in what she needed to do, and before she knew it, she was stepping through the hole and falling into the sea below.

Once Rebecca was in the freezing sea, "well, wasn't that foolish. Why in the world would I go through an open window just to find myself freezing cold in the ocean waters? I am not a very good swimmer. What am I supposed to do? Am I to die here? I made a big mistake in trusting that woman. What was I thinking? They are going to think I am mad and suicidal," she said as she was trying to keep herself from drowning.

Chapter 21

Connor was standing by the rocks just below Dunnottar Castle and close to the water's edge looking out to the sea, as he was thinking of the future that was to come, of the woman he was to meet and shortly after marry, when he heard a splash pulling him out of his thoughts. He stood and walked to the edge of the water, but he couldn't see what it was, so he went further into the water with the need to know what made that large splash, and to his horror, he saw a woman panicking to keep afloat in the water, so he immediately swam out to her and wrapped his arm around her chest and pulled her close to his side.

"Hold on, no move. Relax yerself and I will pull ye to shore."

Rebecca did not hesitate and immediately did as the man said, and when she glanced at the man's face, she knew instantly who he was. It was him – Connor, she was sure of it.

Once Connor had Rebecca on shore, he looked at her and thought, *strange, what garments is she wearing? They are no…right.*

Rebecca was in a panic, as she was coughing up the water that made it into her lungs, and when she looked at the man again, she was not wrong, it was him. "It's you," she said through chattering teeth. "Oh my God, it's you. I'm really here," she said looking around, shaking uncontrollably. She did it. "I'm here," turning back to look at him, "it's you," she was saying until she saw the confusion on Connor's face. "Forgive me. I do not know how I found myself in the water. I have no memory of how I got there. The only thing I can remember was seeing your face. I thought it was a dream though."

"Nae lass, tis no dream. Tis real, I am here. Come, let me get ye to the castle so we can get ye dried. Ye are shivering and yer teeth are chattering," he said as he stood and reached his hand out to help her up.

Rebecca put her hand in his and as she was about to allow Connor to help her up, she stopped and pulled her hand away. "No, I cannot go to the castle. I don't have much time." *I cannot tell him the truth. He will think I am mad.*

"My Lady, ye will get a death of cold if ye no come to the castle and get into something dry," Connor said with concern.

Rebecca shook her head as she wrapped her arms around herself, "No, Connor, I cannot go inside. No one but you must know I am here."

"Lass, ye speak mad. Ye must come to the castle or ye will die," he said, not understanding why those words scared him so.

Looking up at Connor, "no Connor, I cannot. I am sorry, but no one must see me."

Connor not understanding her reasons, decided to sit next to her on the ground. He pulled his tartan from around him and wrapped it around her to give her warmth, when it hit him, "lass, how do ye know my name?" he asked cautiously, fearing she was a spy. "Are ye an English spy? Yer speech is English, but no one I heard before."

Old woman, you sent me here, and now that I am here what am I to say? Do I tell him what I know or remain silent? Rebecca thought, then remembered what the old woman told her, *when you leave, he will not remember meeting you.* With that, Rebecca decided to tell Connor the truth.

Sighing, "I know your name because I know you," she said and saw Connor was about to ask, "no, please let me explain," she said, and Connor nodded in agreement, so Rebecca continued, "I am not from this time. I am from the future. I am here because an old woman sent me here. She said I needed to see and speak to you, that when I do you will recognize me," she said then stopped and turned away from him, *how am I to tell him what I need to tell him? She said he will not remember when I leave, so what the hell.*

"I know your name because I have dreamed about you."

"About me, aye. Why do ye dream about me," Connor asked with astonishment.

"That is a long story, one I don't have time to tell you and I am not English, I am American. I am from America," she said, then with hesitation, "Connor, I am the woman you are to meet and marry…reborn. In my time, you came to me in spirit and reminded me of who I was and who you were, and of the love we once shared…what you will share. I fell in love with you, a man I've never met," she said as she stared out to sea. Rebecca turned to look directly into Connor's eyes, "Connor, you are my heart and soul. I belong to you as you belong to me, but you will not know me until later in your future. The woman you are to marry, you will love with such fierce you…you will love very much."

As Connor listened to this woman, the words she spoke were mad, yet, at the same time, for some odd reason, her words had a ring of truth, and God forgive him, for some reason he believed her. "I am no sure what to say or do with what ye said. For some reason, I believe ye. What am I to do then?"

"There is nothing for you to do. I am only here to tell you this and then I must return,"

Connor for a long moment just sat there staring at this woman, this beautiful woman who did something to his heart…*love? Could tis be? How can I love a woman I just met? Nae, tis no possible.* But he knew it was, because with how he was feeling, how could he doubt it, and then, "ye can no leave me, no now. No when I feel as I do," he pleaded.

"I am sorry Connor, but I must return…now," Rebecca said as she stood up.

"What do ye mean return? Where and how are ye to return?" Connor asked with confusion.

Rebecca at first wasn't sure either until she saw the sea in her mind. "You must return me to the place you found me."

"No!" he said as he stood up. "Ye will drown."

"No, I will not. I am protected. As soon as you return me, I will return to my time."

It was against all he believed, but something said to do what she said. "Aye, I will do what ye ask, but I no like it."

Connor took Rebecca back to the place he found her, and once she was floating safely on her back he returned to the shore, and after a few moments he had to go back and check on her, and when he did, Rebecca was gone. "How tis possible?"

"With my help, tis is," the old woman said.

Connor turned and swam back to shore to find the old woman standing at the shore waiting for him with a smile on her face. "Who are ye?" Connor asked.

"I am a friend. She is safe and ye will see her again," the old woman said, and then she was gone.

After the shock of the woman disappearing before him wore off, Connor looked around and couldn't remember what he was doing there or why he was wet. "What happened?" he whispered, then shrugged his shoulders and turned and started back to the castle with no memory of what happened.

Once Rebecca returned to her time, she was where she was standing before the old woman arrived, in a room of a ruined castle looking out to the sea, with no memory of what happened. Once Rebecca finished her tour of the castle, she felt nothing special, nor did she remember Connor's spirit was with her. It wasn't until much later when she felt him while lying in bed, as bits and pieces of her memory began to return of their time together at the castle, and his presence was stronger than it ever was before. She felt protected with him by her side.

The following morning when Rebecca returned to Dunnottar Castle she arrived at six in the morning before anyone else was around and found herself being pulled in a different direction than the one she wanted to go to, and before she knew it, she was somewhere deep beneath the castle, with the only light she had to see was from small gaps in the ceiling above. It was a large and open space, with there being nothing special about it as she moved slowly in a small circle, taking in her surroundings when a particular spot caught her eye. On the wall that faced west was a small circle of light and when Rebecca approached the spot, she noticed there was something carved in one of the stones, and on closer inspection, she found a Raven with the letter Z in the center, and then, to her shock and surprise she saw her name carved on the Raven's wing.

"My name? How is this possible and why is it there?" Rebecca shook her head, "no, this is impossible, it must be someone else."

"Aye, but tis ye it is. That is yer name," said a woman.

Rebecca spun around when she heard the voice and found an old woman of about sixty standing near the entryway. The woman was a bit shorter than Rebecca and had a pointy nose with slanted eyes and a small heart-shaped mouth. "Who are you?" Rebecca asked, then turned back to the wall with her name on it. She pointed at her name, "how is this me? It looks to have been carved a long time ago," she asked.

The old woman smiled and said, "ah, but ye know what I say is true. He wrote yer name knowing ye would come. Tis ye know, what ye see tis true. Yer highlander, as ye have called him."

Rebecca stood staring at the woman for a long moment shocked by what she said, knowing what she said was true. "Is it possible for us to be together in this life?" she asked.

"Tis true if ye wish it. All ye need to do is step through that doorway," pointing at the spot with the raven on it.

"What happens…no," she said shaking her head. "I cannot go back in time. That is not my place. I will never survive there. I know this. No matter how much I may want to, I cannot."

"Ye can. No to live there, tis no yer place, this is true, but to help him, yer Connor. Yer highlander if ye wish it."

Standing there in utter shock, at first, Rebecca couldn't find any words in response to what the old woman said, and then thought, *can I do this? Do I want to do this?* "I don't know…wait," realizing who the old woman might be after learning about the Fae – fairies actually exist, "you are Fae, aren't you?"

The old woman smiled, "tis true, I am Fae, and ye, ye are Druid born and have the power in ye, and ye know ye can, and ye know ye want to."

What? Druid? she thought. "Druid? No, I am not a druid, but I know I was a Druid Priestess in a past life. Yes, I do, I've thought of nothing else but wanting to be with Connor, to live as his wife after learning about him and what he's done to be with me. With the love he has for me…I want him to be here with me in this life. I know I cannot live in his time…how? What do you mean?"

"Walk through the doorway and ye shall see, and when ye return, so will he."

"Is this your power?"

"Yes and no, tis yers and mine put together."

Okay, this woman is mad. Why am I believing this? Because you want it more than you are willing to admit. Sighing, "if I walk through and enter his time dressed as I am, I will be strange to them," Rebecca said with raised eyebrows as she waved her hand up and down to indicate the clothes she was wearing.

"No worry, I will be there in his time waiting for ye to take ye to him."

"Well, I cannot say I am surprised, after all, for you, this has already happened hasn't it." Rebecca said and when she saw the old woman raise an eyebrow she said, "never mind. What will I feel when I walk through? I've been reading a lot of books about women traveling through time with the help of a Fae in Scotland —"

The old woman laughed as she cut Rebecca off. "Ah lass, tis true, did ye no think why and who was directing ye towards those books."

"Well, yes, I did believe the Fae was involved, but I didn't know how or why."

The old woman smiled, "lass, I have lived in this world a long time and have inspired these stories ye have read. Well, no, tis no just I, but tis of no matter," she said waving her hands in the air, "tis no matter, are ye ready my dear?"

Sighing, she said, "what will I feel?"

"Ye will feel nothing but as if ye walked into another room and ye will feel a shift under yer feet as if ye were on one of yer elevators."

Hum, interesting. "Okay, I guess I am as ready as I am going to be."

"Then think of him as ye put yer hands on the stone on each side of the raven with yer name, and once ye feel the shift, ye will walk through and I will be there on the other side waiting for ye, and when ye are ready, I will take ye to him.

"What year?"

"All will be given to ye once ye are there."

Rebecca nodded and did as the old woman said. When she felt the shift, she walked through the stone wall and when she arrived on the other side, she was standing in seventeenth-century Scotland. As Rebecca looked around, she noticed she was on the east side of the castle overlooking the beautiful green countryside, and from what she could tell, it appeared to be mid-morning. There was a soft breeze, and she could hear the ocean waves splashing against the cliff and rocks below.

"There ye be. I have been expecting ye," said the old woman.

Chapter 22

When Rebecca turned around, she saw the old woman she just left in the twenty-first century looking exactly as she did when she left her in the twenty-first century. "You look the same in this time as you do in mine."

"Am I now, I thank ye then. Now, put these clothes on, then I will take ye to the castle to see yer highlander."

Rebecca took the clothes feeling excited, yet nervous at the same time knowing she was going to see Connor, the man she's only known from her visions and dreams, in flesh and blood. She took the clothes and looked around for a place to change, but there was none. "Here? You want me to change my clothes here?" she asked.

The old woman just looked at Rebecca with a sly smile.

"Of course, you do. Very well then." Rebecca went into the forest and behind a tree, she put on the gown the old woman gave her. It was large enough that she was able to put it on over her own clothes but had to remove her coat. She had to fold down her top to make sure it didn't show around the neckline. Once she was ready, she emerged from the trees and saw the old woman raise her brow in question. "What?" Rebecca asked.

"Give me yer clothes so I can hide them," the old woman said.

"I still have my clothes on, and I hid my coat behind a tree."

The old woman shook her head, "very well. Let us be off then," and together they headed to the castle.

When Rebecca approached the castle entrance, she saw how immaculate it was, it wasn't at all the ruin she just came from. She also noticed, instead of steps, there was a bridge that took her to the tower, and she noticed there were guards on each side of the entrance. Rebecca was surprised after they reached the entrance that the guards waved them through without question. *Well, she is obviously known here,* she thought. Just then, the old woman looked at Rebecca as if she heard her thoughts, but Rebecca only shrugged her shoulders as if it didn't matter.

As they approached the main entrance into the castle, Rebecca was suddenly nervous. "How are you going to explain me, not to mention my accent?" she asked.

"Aye, well, I am bringing ye to Lord Keith as a healer who is mute," she said with a smile and a little chuckle.

"A healer? A mute? Really?" Rebecca said with irritation, although she knew she wouldn't receive an answer. "Very well. Wait. Lord Keith? You mean Connor, don't you? Is he ill?" Rebecca asked with surprise, as well as excitement and a little worried. "He's ill," she asked again.

"Aye, tis so. I thought ye could help him before he moves to the next life. Child, he is old now, and his time is upon him. Ye are here to help him let go of this life so he will move on to the next. Ye, Rebecca, who was his Heather can show him a future he can have with ye."

"Do you really think I can do this? How will he know I am…was his Heather?"

"Because ye have invaded his dreams, and this will allow him to recognize ye. At first, he will think ye a dream, one of many."

"Yes, I believe I understand," and she did, she was aware of those dreams, as she had been a part of them. "Alright, let us do this."

Rebecca was surprised at how easy it was to gain entrance into the castle and how they were able to make it to the outside of the laird's bedchamber door. Once Rebecca and the old woman were at the door, Rebecca had a severe case of butterflies. She put her hand over her stomach and then her chest and said, "are you sure about this?"

The old woman who was standing right next to Rebecca said, "aye, I am. Are ye ready?"

Shrugging her shoulders Rebecca said, "as ready as I'll ever be."

With that, the old woman opened the chamber door, and together they walked in. When Rebecca saw the room, in particular, the window and the chair next to it, she knew this room, it was the same room she saw in her dreams and visions. When Rebecca looked at the bed where Connor was lying, there was a rush of mixed emotions she couldn't understand, and they overwhelmed her. "This is the place I've seen," Rebecca whispered.

The old woman smiled and then turned her attention to Connor. "Connor, I bring ye a guest," she said.

"Old woman, I am in no mood for a guest. Send them away," he yelled with a rough voice, not looking at the old woman.

The old woman motioned for Rebecca to speak, but Rebecca shook her head no. Just then, Connor opened his eyes, and when his eyes rested on Rebecca, he gasped and Rebecca said, "Connor it is I."

"No, I am dreaming. Tis no possible."

Rebecca laid her hand on Connor's arm, then being unable to resist, she moved her hand and started stroking his face. Connor's eyes again flew open and said, "ye can no be real. Yet, ye feel real. How can this be?" he said turning towards the old woman, but the old woman was gone, so he closed his eyes again, hoping the dream would go away.

In a shaky voice Rebecca said, "it's me. God, I can't believe I am here with you." Unable to resist, she sat on the edge of the bed, "Connor, please look at me?"

Connor opened his eyes again, but all he could do was stare at Rebecca, and when he finally found his voice he said, "tis you," and reached up with shaking hands and touched Rebecca's face. He had to feel her, to know she was real. "My Heather, but no Heather. Ye are her…Rebecca," he said. Connor gently caressed Rebecca's chin, as tears started to fall.

Rebecca's heart broke at the sight of Connor's tears. Not understanding why, but only there was a need, she laid down next to Connor and wrapped her arms around him, and he wrapped his arms around her. Rebecca rested her head on his chest and for a while, she just listened to his heart beating before she said, "I love you, Connor, I always have, and I always will." Why she said this, she didn't know, but it felt right. At her words, Connor tighten his hold on Rebecca and cried like a baby, as did she. Rebecca kept saying over, and over again, "I am here. I am sorry. I am so sorry. Forgive me. Please forgive me. If I had known, I would never —"

Connor put his hand over her mouth to quiet her, "tis, no yer fault, ye grieved for me, and it was the only way to end yer pain. I know this because when I learned of yer death, I too wanted death to take me. No matter how hard I tried, I would no die. I lived," shaking his head, "nae, I barely lived. Our connection…dreams helped me. How are ye able to be here?" Connor finally asked.

Rebecca raised her head at his question, "the old woman brought me here from the future…my time," she said, then turned to the place she left the old woman and saw she was no longer in the room and was alone with Connor. "Well, she seems to have left us alone," she said, turning back to Connor.

"I am glad she did. Let me look at ye. Ye do no look like my Heather, but ye are. Ye are just as beautiful, if no more."

"Connor, as Heather, I did you wrong. If you can forgive —" Connor cut her off by placing his hand over her mouth, but Rebecca removed his hand, "no, this must be said. Forgive me for causing you so much pain, and if you can accept me as I am now, then when you are reborn in my time, find me. Find me, and we will be together once again."

"Will ye," choking on his words, "will ye kiss me?" Connor asked.

Rebecca smiled, then leaned down and placed her lips on his, and when she did, Connor grabbed her head and pressed her lips firmly against his and kissed her long and hard. Rebecca was shocked by his strength, but once he kissed her, she relaxed into his kiss, rejoicing in the feel of him. It felt – right.

Once Connor broke the kiss, he looked into Rebecca's eyes, looking for anger, but instead of anger, he only found joy. "Aye, if God wills it, I will find ye then. This I promise ye here on my death bed."

To hear 'on my death bed' caused Rebecca to flinch, then tears began to fall down her face. "Nae, do no cry for me. Ye are here, at my last hours, I could no have wished for anything more," Connor said caressing her face.

Then, there was a knock on the door, along with the voice of the old woman, "Rebecca, we must go now. Lady Keith comes. Tis best to be gone before she arrives."

Rebecca turned to the old woman, "she believes I am a healer…" Rebecca stopped and looked at Connor, "no, you are right. Any woman will know there is more here than they believe. I'm sorry Connor, but I must leave you now. Know that I love you and will be waiting for you in my time."

Connor grabbed Rebecca to pull her to his chest, needing to hold her one last time before letting her go. "As I love ye. I will find ye in yer time. Wait for me, please Rebecca," he said with hope and desperation.

"I will."

"Now Rebecca, we must be on our way," the old woman said again. Reluctantly, Rebecca pulled out of Connor's arms and left his chambers, then followed the old woman down the hall and out the way they came and back to her time.

Chapter 23

<u>Connor</u>

It's been a few days since Connor received the visit from Rebecca, and he couldn't recall a day he ever felt such joy and love that gave him a sense of peace. When Connor took his last breath, he knew he would see Heather again, as well as taking the last words he received from the Fae.

"Connor, tis yer time. Once ye are gone, ye will have a choice. What ye choose, will make a great difference to yer future and Rebecca's. Heed what I say, find Rebecca in the future. Ye must know and understand who she is, to do so will be a great sacrifice ye must make. To do so, will give ye great rewards.

"Old woman, ye talk in riddles."

The old woman smiled, "mark my words. Choose wisely," she said, then she was gone.

When Connor released his last breath, he found himself in a dark place except for a speck of light, then he heard, *come, Connor, we have been waiting for ye.* Connor looked to see where he needed to go, but he could only see darkness, but then he saw other specks of light that were moving away from him, so he decided to follow those lights as he heard, *ye have a choice to make, but first, ye must see yer life as we've seen it, and the way other's seen it. Ye will also see Heather and then Rebecca, then after, a choice will need to be made.*

Next, Connor found himself in a place where he saw his life and as he saw his life unfold, he nodded in agreement with what he saw. What he saw was the decisions he's made, the decision Heather made and the reason she took her life. He saw his life after Heather's death and those around him, then he was shown Heather, now as Rebecca, of her life in the twentieth century and twenty-first century. He saw her pain, her suffering, and her lack of finding love. Next, he saw the love she believed she found, and from there, he watched until he saw Rebecca remembering her life as Elizabeth Massey.

"Now ye must choose. Two choices: one, ye chose to be reborn in the twentieth century like Rebecca and wait until it's time to find her. With time, ye will find her. Or ye can remain here and watch over her until the time comes for her to remember yer life together. If she chooses ye, ye can return to her by being reborn."

Connor stopped, "wait, reborn…ye said if I choose this over being reborn, how can I return to her then?" he asked.

"As spirits in this realm, time does not exist. Ye can do this, then when it's time to return, ye can be reborn. Ye can choose the time ye wish to be reborn, but ye will still have to find her. There is another way, but tis difficult and rarely done. Ye can return as a walk-in. This is when a soul in a current body is no longer needed, and a new soul can take over the body and the life of that person. If ye choose this, ye will have full memory of yer life as Connor and all ye see here. Tis will be a gift granted to ye. Tis is rare, and not offered to many, only to a selected few."

"I know what I will choose."

Rebecca – Dunnottar Castle Scotland

When Rebecca walked through the wall and arrived back in the twenty-first century, she took a moment to gather herself after what she experienced during her time with Connor in the seventeenth century. When she was ready, she went to gather her stuff but noticed they weren't where she left them. Rebecca turned in a circle trying to find where her stuff had gone when she noticed a man. A very tall man with long dark hair.

"Hello," she said.

The man stood from where he was kneeling and turned to where he heard a woman's voice and when he saw her, he thought, *why is she so familiar? Have I seen her before?*

When Rebecca saw this man, her mouth dropped open, it was him, Connor. *How can this be,* she thought, but then realized it wasn't Connor, but a man who looked a lot like him.

When he saw the startled look on the woman's face he said, "I am sorry, is this yours?" he asked, holding up her bag.

Rebecca noticed from his voice he was Scottish and said, "yes, they are. I am sorry, I stepped away not thinking anyone else would be here this early."

The man raised his eyebrow, "early? It's nearly mid-day," he said. "Where did you go, for you to lose track of time?" he asked, then realized he was being rude. "Forgive me, my name is Connor," he said putting out his hand.

You've got to be kidding me! Connor? It cannot be, Rebecca thought as she took his offered hand. "I'm Rebecca."

As soon as their hands touched, a spark flew between them in recognition, along with flashes of memories of their lives together in the seventeenth century, there, at Dunnottar Castle.

Rebecca stumbled, but Connor caught her and steadied her. "Tis ye, isn't it?" he said, with his Scottish brogue from a time past.

Rebecca was shocked and stumbled over her words as she tried to speak, and when she finally found her voice she said, "yes. How can this be? I just left you in the seventeenth century." Although Rebecca asked the question, she knew it was possible, that it was the truth.

For a long moment, Connor could only look at Rebecca, unable to believe his eyes, "aye, did ye know tis was the day?"

"Yes and no. Why is your speech…accent now a stronger Scottish brogue than it was before?" she asked.

"I don't know. Maybe tis when we touched and everything came flooding back," he said, then with realization, *Rebecca, his Heather, but no his Heather. Tis her, who came to me.* Without thinking, Connor grabbed Rebecca and took her in his arms, and to his happy surprise, she didn't resist him and fell into his arms. After holding her for a few moments, he pulled away only enough to lean down and kiss her and she returned the kiss with the same fierceness he was giving her.

"I see ye both found each other," said the old woman.

Startled, Connor and Rebecca quickly broke away. "Forgive us Fae, we did no expect anyone, let alone ye," Connor said.

"Apparently no," she said smiling. "Well, now comes the time for ye to choose."

Connor and Rebecca looked at each other, confused as to what the Fae could mean.

"Nae, of course, ye have no idea," she said, shaking her head. "Allow me to explain to ye. Rebecca, ye have returned to the seventeenth century to see Connor on his death bed, then returned to find Connor as he is now," she said, motioning with her arm to Connor. "If ye choose, ye can walk through that portal together," pointing to the wall Rebecca had just walked through, "and merge with who ye were as Connor and Heather on the day ye were both married. A chance for ye Rebecca to make right the wrong in taking yer life, tis changing the course of what happened when ye do, or ye can both remain here in the twenty-first century, remaining as ye are."

Rebecca and Connor looked at each other shocked at the possibility. Will they return to seventeenth-century Scotland as man and wife, or will they remain in the twenty-first century and create a new life together? This was a decision neither of them expected to have to make.

Rebecca has a life in the twenty-first century. She has her daughter's and a grandson; can she leave them? It's not that she hadn't thought about it. She knew, for some reason deep down it was possible, but could she do it? Could she leave her daughters?

Connor was watching Rebecca very carefully and knew what was happening and remembered where he was before he returned. He was in the spiritual realm. *Ah, aye, I had forgotten. Tis a decision to be made by Rebecca no me. No matter her decision, I shall accept whatever she chooses.*

Rebecca looked at Connor then at the Fae, "I do not belong in the past. This is my time and my place. I have a purpose here, and here is where I need to be," she said then turned to Connor.

"Aye love, then this is where we will remain."

The Fae smiled, "tis the right decision, and Rebecca, I will see ye again," the Fae said, and then she was gone.

Rebecca turned to Connor, "I cannot believe we are together."

"Aye love. We will be together for eternity. Where do ye wish to live?"

"Oh, I have not thought about that. My life is in Arizona and your life is here, how can we make this work? I want to be able to visit my daughter's if I choose to live here, but will that be possible?"

Connor smiled, "aye, tis…it is. In this life, I am very well off and can support ye…you if need be."

"Your words, you are changing from past to present…again."

"Yes, it appears I am adapting to this time."

Rebecca smiled, "I love Scotland and would love to live here…with you."

Stretching out his hand, "then take my hand and let us go home."

Rebecca took Connor's hand and together they left Dunnottar Castle to his home where they lived a happy and flourished life.

The End.

Acknowledgements

Joan Scibienski is a true Psychic for over 30 years and was a great help to certain part of my book. To know more about Joan please visit her websites listed below and her books, The Ariana Series and You Were Born Psychic. Published by Flint Hills Publishing.

Joan L Scibienski
Ariana Series.

Joan L Scibienski
You Were Born Psychic

Please check out her website.
www.intuitivedirections.net
www.channelingeq.com